MW01713788

WHAT YOU NEED

ALSO BY ELIZA CLARK

Miss You Like Crazy

WHAT YOU NEED

A NOVEL

ELIZA CLARK

A Patrick Crean Book

Somerville House Publishing
Toronto

Copyright © 1994 by Eliza Clark

All rights reserved. No part of this publication may be reproduced or transmitted in any form or by any means—electronic or mechanical, including photocopy, recording or any information storage and retrieval system—without written permission from the Publisher, except by a reviewer who wishes to quote brief passages for inclusion in a review.

Canadian Cataloguing in Publication Data

Clark, Eliza
What you need

"A Patrick Crean Book"
ISBN 1-895897-11-4 PB ISBN 1-895897-13-0 HC

I. Title.

PS8555.L355W5 1994 C813'.54 C94-930177-9
PR9199.3.C53W5 1994

Design: Gordon Robertson
Cover photograph: Barbara Cole
Author photograph: Barbara Cole

Printed in Canada

A Patrick Crean Book

Published by Somerville House Publishing,
a division of Somerville House Books Limited:
3080 Yonge Street, Suite 5000, Toronto, Ontario M4N 3N1

Somerville House Publishing acknowledges the financial assistance of the Ontario Publishing Centre, the Ontario Arts Council, the Ontario Development Corporation, and the Department of Communications.

Excerpts from this novel were previously published in Shift *and* Quarry.

The author is grateful for the support of the Ontario Arts Council and the Canada Council.

You Can't Always Get What You Want
– The Rolling Stones

WHAT YOU NEED

ONE

IF WISHES came true, Terrence "Buddy" Whelper would be a butterfly who lived for the day. A man with elbow room and peace of mind, who slept alone because he wanted to. He had fallen head over heels and picked himself up again. He threw himself out into the world like a boomerang, looped solitary back to himself.

His former wife, Cheryl, lived far enough away now that he never had to worry about running into her at the supermarket. Even after they'd separated, they had tended, out of stubborn habit, to shop at the same times. When Cheryl would catch him fondling a lush grapefruit or a hard cucumber, she'd un-dam a flood of curses that always seemed to be perched on the tip of her tongue. Mothers clamped their hands over their tykes' ears and Buddy abandoned his shopping cart and sprinted for the Winn Dixie's automatic doors. Wild-eyed, the back of his neck aflame, his mashed toes limping his gait, Buddy knew he looked ridiculous—possibly frightening.

"Cheryl," he'd yell, "we once had love in common. We were lit from the inside like Japanese lanterns on a moony night."

"That doesn't compute with me," his ex would holler back. "A good marriage isn't a cinch. Counseling has taught me I was crazy for a peckerwood."

Buddy would scramble behind the fuzz-covered wheel of his Ford pickup, his breath coming tight and wheezy, a cruel stitch jabbing his side, and grope for the bourbon under the seat. There was always an element of truth to what his ex-wife said, but mostly Buddy was hightailing it across the parking lot before she got to the point and began pitching whatever canned goods were in her vicinity. The small children, who couldn't hear much, ducked down and judged him, he bet, for the worse.

His marriage to Cheryl hadn't been a total loss. They'd lived quite comfortably. Unlike him, Cheryl had always had a job. Most recently she was a headhunter for a major advertising company where Buddy thought she made a whopping salary considering what she did—which as far as he could tell was talk on the phone all day and hold mysterious closed-door meetings. They lived firmly entrenched in the suburbs, in a house so big Cheryl insisted on speaking to Buddy via an extensive intercom system, which he consistently threatened to rip from the wall. Between them, her mostly, they'd produced a sizable nest egg that more and more Buddy felt to be a pain in his ass. Over the years too, Cheryl had somehow disassembled him, inspected the pieces like germs under a microscope, and then put him together again helter-skelter, anywhichway.

Terrence "Buddy" Whelper in the original sense no longer existed. When he really thought about it, the transformation had come upon him inch by inch, growing as relentlessly as a weed under the constant watering of Cheryl's tears. Tears she'd shed accusingly, and seemingly unstoppably, as a direct result of something he'd said or had not said. He felt he was an uncomplicated, even simple, human being and what he didn't want was to hurt her feelings, or anybody else's for that matter. Bewildering as it was to him, Buddy soon learned to read Cheryl Jean Hebb's emotional barometer and acclimatize himself accordingly. If she indicated rain, he greased himself for an icy downpour; if it was to be fair skies, he got naked. He responded swiftly and professionally to hint and innuendo. He nipped hormonally triggered conniptions in the bud.

There were times Buddy was sure Cheryl's wailing would bring the police to his door, whereupon she'd convince them to arrest him for being emotionally plugged and, further, lackluster, as she was always accusing him of being. Could be he was, because when she began her tirade the only thing Buddy could think to do was stick his fingers in his ears and recite aloud scenic spots in America he hoped to visit before he died. "The Grand Canyon, Disney World, Las Vegas," he'd tell her. Cheryl would cry, pounding her girlish fists into a pillow. "Weeki Wachee Springs, Graceland, Niagara Falls, Dollywood, the Empire State Building," he'd say through the name calling and plate throwing. But when, after a brief spell of giving the cat her tongue, Cheryl announced a plan to withhold from him her pleasure palace, all reasonable doubt left his mind.

Buddy had no idea why then he would suddenly be crazy for his wife. He'd come up with such inventive wooings he thought he should write a book. He sucked each one of Cheryl's toes and licked the grooves in between with abandon. He went for secret, hairless places untouched by the sun—the insides of elbows, the backs of knees, the nape and navel—showering them all with heartfelt, sloppy kisses. He moaned. He crooned love words and what he hoped would be inspirational thoughts deep into her ear, moistly naming Kama, Eros and Cupid. Cheryl, likening him to a pig rooting for truffles, after many fruitless nudgings away, gave in with a tired sigh, and Buddy wallowed and wallowed.

Daily, Buddy found himself speaking contrary to what he meant. Yes, he told Cheryl to everything. He enjoyed shopping at the mall, chemical logs in their fireplace, mushroom gravy on the whole of her culinary repertoire. The more he hated a thing, the louder he proclaimed his admiration for it. That went for Cheryl too. The more she claimed he didn't love her, the more adamantly he struggled to prove his affection. It had all become so confusing.

Her instincts told her one thing, but he was trying to convince her, to convince himself, of another. He married her, for better or worse, to end the debate.

Buddy held a bunch of odd jobs—short-order cook, usher at a movie theater, car salesman. At the Chrysler dealership, he answered to the name Terry, which the other salesmen convinced him was a hipper, more college-educated-sounding name than Buddy—one that would reflect well in his commission checks. Only the petite secretary, Janine, called him Buddy because she thought it was cute, a grown man having a little boy's name.

He grew used to all manner of cramps, tics, spasms and rashes affecting various parts of his body at any given time. His body was rebelling against the way he was living his life. A hard fight began within himself. As a matter of self-preservation, Buddy hooked on to relaxation techniques such as yoga, transcendental meditation, whale music, lapping wave sounds and the drumming of rain, shiatsu massage, aromatherapy. He invented his own version of primal screaming. He came up with, then perfected, a number of deep-breathing exercises meant to combat stress. Stress is what Buddy believed was sinking him into his personal quicksand.

Generally, the exercises involved doing something that required such nitpicky concentration that he had no time to worry about anything other than the task at hand. His favorite was a complicated method of breathing that involved inhaling through each nostril separately, then exhaling through his mouth with audible force. When Buddy found himself doing exactly the opposite—inhaling through his mouth and exhaling nostril by nostril—he tried not to get too down on himself since it would defeat the purpose of the stress-buster.

Because the exercises seemed to be working wonders, Buddy ventured a step further and devised strict rules of conduct for himself. He hoped that by eliminating all chance and happenstance from his daily life, he'd be empowered and remain in complete control of whomever this Terry was he'd become. He taught himself to be aware of his every gesture: recognize it, modify it, control it. He ate sweet foods only on the right side of his mouth, everything else on the left. He wore his shirts in alphabetical order by the manufacturer's label beginning on Day 1, which was Monday. He ought to get back to nature, he thought, so made it a daily habit to smell a flower, walk on grass, or at the very least stamp on an ant with his shoe if it was a particularly bad day. He bought a rowing machine and used it.

Sadly, words began to lose their meaning for him. Sometimes he had no idea what he was talking about but was aware, as through a fog, of his lips moving. He would be stammering halfway through a sentence, halfway through a long word, and give up on it to hum a Jimmy Buffett tune instead. Other times, a word would come into his head and lie there like a sick dog on the road until he paid it some attention. When he'd finally think of a way to incorporate the word into a useful sentence, the relief that followed its leaving his tongue made him practically whoop. "Untruculent," he would say, his body heat rising, "roustabout, kumquat, poodle." Daily he tried to include one word from the outskirts of his vocabulary in a viable sentence. "This car's engine is a lollapalooza."

Buddy also began to drink. He considered alcohol a kind of necessary truth serum. Every two or three months he would get quietly plastered and tell Cheryl he was not the man she thought he was. He would take off the patterned boxer shorts she liked him to wear and put on a pair of white Fruit of the Loom briefs with shot elastic to prove it. He would stand before her drunk, and mostly naked, and announce that this was who he was—the real T. Buddy Whelper, like it or lump it. Cheryl would raise an eyebrow, gently chew the end of her pencil while she considered him, then go back to her paperwork.

Their marriage ended shortly after Buddy decided to remake himself in his old image once and for all. He began with a five-day juice fast, also known as an elimination diet, which was perfect because he intended to eliminate more than fat. He was going after years of wishy-washy pandering and useless beating around the bush. His new motto was Float like a Butterfly, Scoot like a Bee. He would strive to be smooth in all matters, diplomatic, and if he could help it, let only the truth pass his lips. He decided also to quit trying to squelch his sexual urges and unshackle the marital chains from his libido.

It had been six or seven months since Cheryl had not been too tired with her job responsibilities to have energy left over for even the laziest lovemaking.

"Cheryl," Buddy would plead with her, "this isn't normal. We are a happily married couple with scented candles and no children to spoil our romantic interludes. We ought to be having sex at least twice a week. Honey, we shouldn't need to sleep. Sleep is for losers and little kids. I see the candy but I can't get the sugar. This is not a sex maniac talking, Cheryl, though you make me feel like one. Bop with me, baby."

"I don't think so," Cheryl would say.

"Please," Buddy would say, begging hopelessly, helplessly too.

"Maybe some other time. I can't tell for sure, but I guess somewhere along the line, the bulk of my passion for you got rerouted into other things. Career, possibly."

"What else?" Buddy asked with sinking esteem.

"You name it," Cheryl said.

Sick with a cold one day, she'd dragged herself away from her work at the office and had come home hoping to crawl into bed and sleep off the worst of it in time for a big meeting the next morning. Unfortunately, the bed had been occupied by a redhead Cheryl thought she recognized from behind the cash at the Winn Dixie. The girl was riding astride Buddy, her young breasts bouncing wildly. Cheryl was surprised, then deeply wounded, to hear her husband yelping with unfamiliar glee.

TWO

BUDDY was thirty-seven years old when he put his metal suitcase onto the seat of his pickup truck and waved good-bye to his wife, who didn't stop blowing her nose long enough to wave back. For all the relief he felt, there was a twinge of guilt somewhere in the midst of him that made him struggle for something to say to her in parting. "Good-bye, Cheryl," he called out, "and no hard feelings."

"Creep!" she yelled back. "Freak of nature! Moron!" and slammed the door.

Buddy waited, the pickup idling noisily beneath him, in case Cheryl might be inspired to add a kinder, more open-ended footnote. He stared at his closed front door, then changed gears and drove himself away.

Out on the highway, some miles later, he pulled up at a roadside zoo to look at a black bear. The sign said LIVE BEAR in peeling paint and Buddy stopped to see it. The bear was the only animal around, although other cages stood empty. The zoo was meant as an attraction to lure people over to the gas station and snack bar beside it, but mostly, it seemed, the cars went by. All day and night the bear breathed exhaust from the highway and lived in a cage so small it couldn't stand without hitting its head on the wire roof. The floor was filthy and the animal, BoBo he was called, stood in matted straw mixed with his own waste and candy wrappers. His feet were ulcerated and his growth stunted. A diet of sodas and donuts tossed to him by visitors had wrecked his health. Buddy watched as a little girl chucked stones at the bear from a slingshot her father had made from a branch. The man held the girl's wrist steady as she took aim, and every time the animal groaned with a hit she jumped up and down, clapping her hands in delight while her father reached into the dirt for another stone. The last thing Buddy saw was that the lock on the cage had rusted shut, it hadn't been opened for so long.

Buddy set up in a one-bedroom apartment in Savannah. He was able to pay half the usual monthly rent by hiring himself out as the building's superintendent slash Mr. Fix-It. The building was eighty years old, and Buddy spent at least part of every day in one of the twenty-four units repairing or replacing something that probably hadn't worked right for years. The two supers before him had been neither mechanically inclined nor ambitious and had let things fall into major disrepair. Buddy, on the other hand, liked fixing things, whether it be electrical problems, plumbing or simple carpentry. He liked the cool, heavy weight of tools in his hands and knowing which was the right tool for the job. They knew him by sight at Guffin's Hardware store, where he regularly went to pick up this item or that gadget he needed. It was always something. Maybe a tenant had let the bathtub overflow and ruined the ceiling plaster in the apartment below, or another had started a fire in the kitchen, another wanted their lock changed to keep out a jealous lover. Punk Guffin would stop whatever he was doing to help Buddy search out the thing he was after. Punk had a big mouth and rambled on his own steam without needing fuel from Buddy to propel him on. Buddy knew about Punk's open marriage, the plastic joints in his knees and the tiny, hot Picasso he'd acquired in the course of his previous job as a loan shark's thumb-breaker. When he pondered himself as a stranger might, Buddy gladdened to see a booze-free, lean-muscled handyman who was mostly useful and unembittered. His stomach was amiable once more and his nightly sleep frolicked with babylike dreams.

The building's landlord, a Greek named Cosmo, knew he'd hit the jackpot with Buddy. In fact, had Buddy ever complained about the minimal rent he was paying, Cosmo would have let him stay for free, so grateful was he to have found him. But Cosmo was a businessman. He showered upon Buddy instead winsome perks—a prime parking spot under a shady tree; an expense account, the monthly bill for which he paid no questions asked; even an outside agency hired to clean the windows so Buddy wouldn't have to. Gestures Cosmo hoped would speak louder than words in telling Buddy he was appreciated.

Which he was. The four-story brownstone had never looked better. People were starting to knock on Cosmo's door, asking about vacancies, willing to pay twice what he was charging the present tenants. Yes, Buddy was worth his weight in gold. Surely Cosmo could close his eyes to the peculiarities, the behavioral quirks that some of the tenants complained were becoming stranger by the minute. After all, Cosmo reasoned, a man left to his own devices, unprissied by a woman's domesticating touch, was bound to be somewhat rough around the edges. It was nothing to get alarmed about. Still, perhaps—and Cosmo made a mental note to do so—he ought to talk to Buddy about his appearance. Buddy could try getting keener about his grooming: pull his hair back into a ponytail; shave his face; maybe splash some cologne into his armpits. Also—here Cosmo would insist—the miner's hardhat and safety goggles had to go unless Buddy was actually fixing something. Even if they came in as handy as Buddy claimed they did, he had to understand he made a bad impression wearing them around everywhere he went. Surely, Cosmo thought, if he held up a mirror, described to Buddy how he looked limping down the building's narrow corridors with his hair wild and frazzy beneath the mining helmet, the flashlight beam from his forehead illuminating the path ahead as he peered through the safety goggles for sprinkles of rodent or insect dung—well, he looked odd, frankly. A fact is a fact. Cosmo would tiptoe, be oily-tongued and delicate, and he sorely hoped Buddy wouldn't be offended by the suggestions.

Buddy had bought the minimal amount of furniture necessary to decorate his apartment, with the only requirements being that the pieces be both functional and comfortable. Instead of posters or starving artists' oil paintings, Buddy had hung his tools in Rubbermaid organizers on his living-room walls where they could be easily seen and gotten at. He'd placed his rowing machine in front of the living-room window to catch a nice breeze while he exercised. Other smaller tools, and nails, clamps, glue, were put in dresser drawers alongside his clothes, since his wardrobe was now nominal. He'd put the TV he'd rescued from the dumpster and repaired himself in the bedroom beside the one item he had splurged on: a self-warming Craftmatic adjustable double bed. He'd seen the bed advertised during the commercial breaks on "American Gladiators," while lying stiffly, disappointedly, on a futon he'd bought after years of trying to talk Cheryl into getting one. It had taken a while, but Buddy could now honestly say he loved his adjustable bed and looked forward to his hours spent in it. He couldn't deny he'd used up more than some restless nights tossing, trying to accustom himself to the position they showed in the commercial, whereby his head and shoulders, legs and feet were raised to form a human V. But now that he was, Buddy felt sorry for people who had to sleep flat as animals in the wild. Too, he was nearly used to clapping off the bedside light by way of The Clapper, a device the bed makers had thrown in as a bonus and which Buddy couldn't get over feeling shy and silly about, although he wasn't sure why since it was as handy as they promoted it to be.

Apart from the bedroom, the next best furnished room was the kitchen because Buddy was teaching himself how to cook. When the knock came on the door, he had just finished marinating the chicken for Aunt Cindy's Lemon Chicken Divine.

THREE

DORENE LATISHA PERNEY heard some shuffling behind the door but when nobody opened it, she knocked again. She had reason to believe the planets and stars had recently aligned against her, because her life was a mess and she couldn't find any other cause for it to have gone downhill so fast. She could add up on her fingers the days ago when her heart was untrampled and Chad Delmonte was still her boyfriend. But Chad had turned out to be a no-good loser, plus dangerous, and she was right to have murdered him. Still, when she let her mind slip, she could hear him singing "Michael, row your boat ashore" sweet as any choirboy, the way he did when they were making love, and she had to admit, despite herself, she ached for his company. How could anybody who timed their thrusts so perfectly with the "jah" part of "hallelujah" be all bad? But that was earlier in their relationship, and Dorene forced herself to stop making romantic what wasn't. Take his coming home every night with lipstick on his collar and her washing it off every morning. Under the hard, unclouded sun the red stains she scrubbed had a glare that made her eyes water. After a while, though, she'd had to admit the sun's shine wasn't to blame for her tears; it was a kind of allergic reaction to Chad's cheating. Her tears fell, glistening on his smooch-soiled collars like dew clinging, just clinging to wild grass the morning after.

Dorene checked the name she'd jotted on a scrap of paper. "Hey, B. Whelper? I know you're in there! I heard pitter-patters." She pounded softly on the door and snapped her gum. "Your name's on my list from the agency. You're not a deaf mute, are you?"

Dorene began gently to twist the doorknob and felt it being grasped and countertwisted with equal force.

"That's all right," Dorene said. "I don't blame you for being suspicious. I might not open the door myself. But it's true that strangers are only people you don't know—if you want to think about it this way: sides of your personality you're not in touch with yet—though that may be too complex psychologically for you to understand. Are you looking at me through that peephole? Do you think that's fair, Whelper? It's kind of sneaky."

"What are you selling?" Buddy blurted out and immediately felt, by virtue of his speaking, that he'd been suckered into something.

"Aha. Don't worry. I saw the sign No Trespassers, No Solicitors. I'm not selling anything and anyway I bet there's nothing you need, right? You have everything your heart desires right there in your L-shaped living room. Sure you do." Dorene smiled at the little glass peephole. "So, B. Whelper?" she said to the fish-eye lens.

"What?"

Dorene took out her gum and plugged it into the peephole.

Buddy stared at nothing, then opened the door.

"Hi," Dorene said. "I won't bite." She noted Buddy's woolly hair and apron and inwardly rolled her eyes. He looked like a cross between Grizzly Adams and Doris Day. Que sera sera. She reached down for her ghetto blaster and the faded pillowcase she'd been keeping upright between her feet and walked into his apartment. Dread formed a lump in Buddy's throat.

It took nerve for Dorene to enter a stranger's place. A stranger who, for all she knew, could be a pervert or insane dope fiend, but she'd come a long way this past week. She'd left behind her the old Dorene full of hope and intact dreams. She'd traded that one in for a harder-bitten model, one equipped to deal with the world's mean streak. And besides, if she was honest about it, chances were good that she was the only killer present.

Buddy gazed the length of the empty corridor, then went inside too. In his experience, one bad move followed another. His first mistake had been to say anything. His second to open the door. A ripple of bad moves, a tidal wave was all he needed to sink him under.

"Close the door, sug," Dorene said from the living room where she'd plunked her coat on the floor. One look around had told her B. Whelper was a bachelor, and she allowed herself a sigh of relief. So far so good. She unwrapped a turkey roll sandwich, thankful for the grumbling return of her appetite, premiering for the first time since she'd done Chad in. With her mouth full, Dorene said, "Excuse me, Whelper, I need to tank up." She pushed Buddy with her free hand into the only chair in the room, hard enough that the attached footrest swung out and the back reclined. Dorene wondered how come men prefer frumpy comfort to good looks in everything except their women.

Buddy half laid in the chair and they met eyes. Dorene saw in Buddy's a Post-it that said *no thank you* to whatever she had to offer. Well, that's too bad, she thought, she wasn't so thrilled herself. But under the circumstances, this was the best plan she had to save her own neck, and plus, start a new life. From now on Dorene was making Dorene her top priority. To hell with being nice. Nice was for people who saw rainbows and forgot about the rain that pelted you first. Dorene had seen enough black skies, enough black eyes, to forget about anything. In her heart, she knew there was no good reason to look up most times. She figured if she saw Heaven she'd know it. Until then she had enough problems with the earth moving under her feet.

"The bedroom's thataway?" she said, pointing with the last of her sandwich. Buddy felt words clambering but they went nowhere of any use. Dorene winked at him. "Don't worry, Whelper. In some ways I'm like a compass." She grabbed her pillowcase and headed for his bedroom.

Buddy stared at the forget-me-nots and strawberries-on-the-vine patterning his apron. He shook his head as though his ears were full of water. "I'm done with females as a bunch," he mustered, then called it out to the one in his bedroom. "I want to fix broken things and know about spices. Please," he said. He had a sad history of befuddlement where women were concerned.

"Close your eyes, Whelper. No peeking now."

Buddy's eyes were closed. He felt the air stir beside him as Dorene walked past. He heard her press a button on the ghetto blaster. Tony Orlando and Dawn launched into "Tie a Yellow Ribbon 'Round the Ole Oak Tree" and Buddy winced through his shut eyes.

"Okay, open them!" Dorene said. "I'm a dynamic Gemini, The Twins. Tests have proven I'm right-brained too, which makes me doubly creative and interesting. Further, a born entertainer. I wanted you to know because I came up with this whole number myself and you might not have believed me otherwise. I'm working at promoting myself in a straightforward, hopefully charming, way because if I don't, who will, right?"

Dorene was wearing a striped prison outfit with a matching striped hat and army boots. She began to sing along with Tony Orlando, loudly topping him note for note, lilt for lilt. She twirled and danced around the living room in front of Buddy. After some heavy stomping in the black boots, she made a big production of taking them off. Then she pretended to frisk herself all over, cupping her breasts, pouting as she touched her crotch. She put her own index finger in her mouth and sucked it. She unzipped the prison top partway to reveal a full, freckled cleavage. It was then Buddy got that she intended to become naked in front of him. He broke into a sweat.

"Whoa," he choked. "I'm Buddy Whelper. Maybe it's a Bill or a Brad Whelper you're after. Wait—I'll get the phone book."

But Dorene was so caught up in the music and her performance that she seemed not to hear Buddy and flung her hat into his lap. She shook out her hair and mashed her hands up through it till it went wild and bedroom-mussed. Perspiration ran in hot rivers down Buddy's sides. With her back to him, Dorene unzipped her top all the way. She slipped off first one shoulder then the other and pretended like she'd gone shy and wanted to cover herself up again before she pitched the top clear across the room, where it landed on the rowing machine. She was wearing a yellow push-up bra, and Buddy made the thematic connection to the song with no trouble, even though his head was fuzzy and he'd begun to pant like a small dog locked in a hot car.

Dorene ran her tongue across her upper lip and narrowed her eyes. She pursed her lips and went, "Oooh." Buddy could tell she was operating from some place else. She mashed her hair more and undid her fly. She turned slightly, flashing him. She dipped and shimmied, teasing Buddy with vistas of tummy, slopes of hip. She sang, "It's been ten long years, do you still want me?" and slid the pants off one firm, rounded cheek then the other, before letting them drop to the floor. She ducked her head through her legs and blew Buddy a kiss, her face fleetingly as pink as his. When she turned again, Buddy saw that there was something written on the front of her tiny, glitzy G-string panties, though he couldn't quite make it out. From where he was it looked like "RENE," and he figured that must be her name.

"Look here, Rene—" he said hoarsely.

But it didn't matter a squib to Dorene. She was mystical. Transposed. She danced around the room, circling her hips, playing up her cleavage by way of specialized shoulder shrugs and upper-arm squeeze-ins. She fingered the front-opening clasp of her bra but saved opening it until the exact second Tony Orlando sang about the ex-con seeing the hundred ribbons around the ole oak tree instead of the maybe one he'd expected. It was then, when the newly freed man understood he could go home again and the whole bus was cheering for him, that Dorene whipped off her bra and shook her breasts with empathetic jubilation the way others might wave a flag. Then it was all over and she pressed Stop on the tape deck.

"Happy Birthday, Whelper, from Ed and Uncle Mac." She was flushed and out of breath, her eyes bright as firecrackers.

"Thank you very much, Rene, but this is a big mistake." Buddy spoke to Dorene's butt as she bent over her coat pockets. He wiped the sweat off his brow and shifted in his seat.

Dorene turned on him with a cigarette dangling from her mouth. "You *are* B. Whelper, right? Did you just call me Rene?" Dorene lit the cigarette with a match, then folded her arms across her bare breasts and puffed.

Buddy went and opened the nearest window, held his face in front of the moist breeze. "It says on your underpants—RENE. I didn't think you'd put someone else's name down there." Buddy pointed loosely to the triangular patch of cloth before his other hand closed over his pointer and brought it down.

Dorene bent to look at her crotch and showed Buddy how the DO part of the embroidery had gotten folded under. "See, Whelper. It's DOrene," she said and right away could have kicked herself. "But actually, you shouldn't believe everything you read. You need to look at facts and the history that leads up to a thing. This string bikini is a loaner. It belongs to one of the girls at the agency—her name's Dorene. Mine's not, though I can see how you'd think it was, logically and all, but it's not. I don't even look like a Dorene, do I? Picture a Dorene. See, it's not me. My name's Abigail."

"Abigail?"

"Abby." Dorene dragged hard on her cigarette.

"Well, I don't know," Buddy said. "That's a lot of names. If you consider Rene, Dorene, Abigail and Abby. I don't know if I can remember all those names."

Dorene stared at him. "What, are you kidding? Oh, for pete's sake, you don't have to remember them all. Just forget about Dorene. There is no Dorene. I'm Abby and you're the wrong Whelper, that's all we need to know." Dorene sat down in the La-Z-Boy and smoked irritably.

"Maybe," Buddy said, "you should call your agency and get them to check the address for you. Explain you were at the wrong place at the right time, which in itself is an easy mistake to make. I'm sure it happens more than we'd guess." Out of the corner of his eye Buddy then caught sight of his lemon chicken on the kitchen counter. He'd forgotten about it but now wanted to get cooking again as though the chicken were a magnet, pulling.

"What time is it?" Dorene asked. She suddenly was so tired she didn't think she'd be able to raise her head from the chair if she tried. It was the same way she felt after her dead boyfriend, Chad, would come home drunk in the middle of the night and try to pick a fight with her about something or, more often, nothing. With beer falsely sweet on his breath, Chad's tongue would lash meaner than ever, his thoughts, such as they were, jealous and cruel. He'd be snarly as a caged animal, too big for any room he was in, striding back and forth knocking things over, tearing at his clothes, and hers. He'd swear vicious names at her, and more and more often, he'd hit her. Then he'd run be sick in the toilet, cursing and coughing, making a bad mess. Dorene would fix coffee in the kitchen. If she wanted to, she could have filled the kettle with her tears and boiled that for water instead. At those times, she hated herself as much as she hated Chad, which went against her nature on both counts. She felt just as sorry for them both too. It was like they'd been cast parts in a terrible play that they had no choice but to act out. Chad would bring her ice cubes wrapped neatly in a dish towel to hold on her face where it would be starting to swell, darkening with blood running under the surface where he'd struck her. He'd wait for her to say something. Maybe—it was all right what he'd done, his temper had gotten away from him was all it amounted to.

"Chad," Dorene would say through her split lip, swallowing blood, "this isn't how love ought to be. We don't have to be romantic, because I know life isn't, but it doesn't have to be this awful either. We're in a rut, a sorry, tarnished groove. You need to find another outlet. I forgive you, but what about jogging up steep hills?"

Dorene had been wrong, though—she hadn't forgiven or forgotten. Nothing had been all right. She hadn't forgiven one punch. Or lipstick-smeared collar. Or tooth knocked loose in her head. And oh, worse. Why else would Chad Delmonte be stiffening in his bathtub?

"It's nearly six."

"Well, that's that. The agency's closed. I guess I'll have to call tomorrow." Dorene was watching the sides of the room close in as though she was looking through the narrowing lens of a telescope. Her stomach tightened and lurched. "Whelper," she said, barely aloud. She could hardly keep her eyes open, the room was tilting.

Buddy had been avoiding looking at Dorene directly since her naked breasts were such a distraction from her face, where he felt he ought to be looking out of politeness. But now he did look over just in time to see her eyeballs roll white and her body limpen in a faint. He took the smoldering cigarette from her hand and tossed it out the open window. When he turned back, her eyelids were fluttering like insect wings. He touched her forehead. He couldn't remember if you were supposed to cool down an unconscious person or warm them up. He did both. He sponged Dorene's wrists and ankles with a wet cloth and then went to get her coat. As he was laying the coat over her, she jolted awake. Before he could react and get out of the way, she karate-chopped his collarbone. She swung her fists through the air and kicked him out of reach like she meant business. Buddy stumbled and she chopped him again on the back of his neck.

"Christ," he gasped. He staggered towards the kitchen. But Dorene was standing perfectly still. Her eyes were blinking rapidly and they followed his path. He was worried that at any second she might leap and fling violence on him again. Buddy spoke to her in a calm, he hoped soothing voice like she was a jumper on a narrow ledge. He told her she'd passed out cold and perhaps she ought to find a hospital. He brought her a glass of orange juice with crushed ice and put it down on the floor near her, but not too close. She was gazing around the room, stunned and disoriented.

"I'm sorry," she said, slumping into the chair. "I guess I thought you were somebody else. I hope I didn't hurt you."

"Fainting's not a sign of anything good," Buddy said. "Brain tumors, diabetes, heart disease, mononucleosis, malaria, the list goes on. There's a hospital only a few blocks from here."

"No. No hospital. Please. If I could just sleep for a little while, I'll be fine. I won't be any more trouble, I promise. You won't even know I'm here."

Buddy didn't see what else he could do. "Drink your juice," he advised lamely.

"Thanks, Whelper. You won't regret it." Dorene drained her glass.

It wasn't long before her mouth dropped open in sleep and Buddy saw the pink tip of her tongue caught between her teeth. He reclined the chair and draped her coat over her, tucking it snug around her shoulders and thighs to keep off drafts. Beads of perspiration glistened along her upper lip and across her brow, and Buddy dabbed them away with the cloth, wondering if, despite what she'd said, he ought to call a doctor. In the end, though, he decided to let her rest and see how the situation looked when she woke up. Maybe stripping was a more tiring thing than was commonly thought. Lord knows, in its own way it had worn him out.

With shaking hands, Buddy put his lemon chicken in the oven and scalloped potatoes enough for two. What he couldn't stop thinking was this was how the worst of his dreams began. He'd be minding his own business when out of nowhere a woman would appear, and before he knew it he'd be turned inside out and backwards. Now here a woman had come out of the blue, knocking on his door with his name on her list. A list of people she was supposed to take her clothes off in front of and wish happy birthday. Why him, after all? Buddy pondered whether there wasn't something about him, some flaw in his character that made him a willing target. But that was paranoid, he decided. Strippers probably went to wrong addresses all the time. They stripped and then they left, went and stripped again at the right place. No big deal. He was probably the only person who'd ever tried to give it a deeper meaning.

Buddy filled the sink with water and shot in some Palmolive. He stacked his dirty dishes carefully and began scrubbing them with a cloth. If he could keep things clean and tidy, he thought, that would help.

FOUR

LOOKING at herself in the mirror over Buddy Whelper's bathroom sink was like looking at her mother and that was enough to make Dorene look away. It was 3 A.M. and she'd startled awake from a nightmare about Chad. In it she was spooning Miracle Whip onto Chad's belly and licking it off as though it was the nicest thing in the world to be doing. Dorene did not plan on being haunted by Chad Delmonte for the rest of her life, and after picking up this and that little bottle or tube took some Pepto-Bismol out of Buddy's medicine cabinet and patted it onto her T-zone, the oily strip of forehead and nose down the center of her face. Her mother always said that in a pinch, Pepto-Bismol was as good at drawing out skin impurities as anything else she'd tried. Her mother had Dorene's same wide-open blue eyes. They were like a map of the roads they'd traveled and indicated just how much time they'd spent chasing down dead ends on the heels of some tall hombre who knew how to tell jokes and embellish his scars. Dorene's eyes got stuck on a man's white smile and went blind to anything darker about him, a trait she'd inherited genetically. Both of them, mother and daughter, thought inside every closed fist was a diamond ring, and they suffered punches that were velvet boxes, the only kind they knew, empty within.

Dorene wasn't better in the hearing department, since her ears pretty much echoed back what she wanted them to hear. Her mother was different. She only had to hear a person say their name, and if she felt like it, she could tell them ten things about themselves they'd know to be secret and true. It was a gift. What the Egyptians called the third eye, except in her mother's case it was the third ear.

When Dorene was seven, her mother went on "Name That Tune" and cleaned up. She won all the money the show's producers were willing to give anybody who could name song titles from teasing blips. Her mother had played the "Hooked-On" series of records over and over for research before she went on television, although she hadn't needed to. She remembered by heart any song she'd ever heard. Dorene sat in the studio audience, taking little bites at her thumbnail as her mother, a former Miss Good Posture, declared with charm and straight back, "I can name that tune in one note." And she had again and again until Dorene was bouncing off her seat into the studio's loftimost heights.

Her mother and a "Name That Tune" cameraman had taken up together for a while afterwards and he'd asked her what she was going to do with all that money she'd won. "Why, I'm going to spend it all on you," her mother had said, because she lived to flirt, and she'd gone out and bought him a Japanese car and a pineapple from Hawaii. "That's to show you I'm not hot air," she'd said as she handed him the keys and a knife. "The world is closer than you think. Whatever you need is right here and attainable." She'd licked juice trickles from the corners of her mouth with jabs of her tongue. The man had looked just right as he sped off in his new sportscar while her mother waved good-bye to him with her single bare hand. "Aloha," she'd said, knowing it meant welcome and farewell, the story of her life.

What the man hadn't lingered to find out was that they didn't need the prize money. They had more money in the bank than "Name That Tune" gives out in a year, in two years, thanks to her mother's ears. For as long as Dorene could recall, people had been willing to pay hard cash for the privilege of knowing what went on in the inner chambers of the miracles that poked out either side of her mother's head.

She heard dead people. For commercial reasons, her mother went by the name Destinee Oracle, which is what Dorene had mostly grown up calling her. There was a sign in the front window of their house that read DESTINEE ORACLE *Natural-Born Psychic, Automatic Writing, Clairaudient. Works with Police. 87% Accurate.* This last statistic her mother had added reluctantly, saying only that it was a sad fact of humanity that people needed numbers to know how good a thing was—look at Bo Derek.

Dorene had called Destinee on the telephone from Chad's apartment right after she'd nixed him to find out if this was one of her mother's "dry spells"—those microscopic interludes when no boyfriend was living with her—and to ask then if she could come hide out for a while. There had been a long pause on the other end after she'd said hello. Dorene had yelled, "Yo, Destinee! Yoohoo, Ma." But her mother had been listening to something else entirely, and it wasn't the ballgame in the background either, which answered Dorene's question about there being a man in the house or not.

As she'd waited, Dorene had sweated it out, wondering if Chad was spilling his guts already from the near beyond, snitching on her, which she knew he'd love to. "Shoot, Destinee Oracle! I can't stick around all day while you put me on hold. If that's Chad Delmonte tying up my line, you tell him nobody does what he did to me and gets away with it. What did he think, that it was all right with me? That I'd get over it? Ha. You know how long I've wanted to be a backup singer. Did he think he could stamp out all my dreams, every lifelong dream of mine, and still have me around to fondle and do laundry? I say plug your ears, Destinee. And you better not look at him neither. You're as bad as me when it comes to a winsome face. Oh, Mama, those blinding white teeth." Dorene hung up finally when it didn't seem her mother was about to say anything in the near future.

All Dorene had ever wanted was three things. To be a backup singer in a band, wearing skimpy clothes with sparkle to them, coordinating her movements with a girl fatter than she was, to make her look petite jiving beside. To marry a man she could eat with a spoon. And to have twin babies, or at least a boy first and then a girl, with pink toes and dimples. It didn't seem like so much to ask when there were people who wanted to fly in space and cure cancer for a living. Dorene had set herself on a direct course towards her goals as soon as she'd figured them out in high school. She was prepared to defend them too, because without a game plan where would she be in the world? How would she ever know she wasn't just spinning around on her own axis, content as a moon but getting nowhere? How could she be sure she was Dorene L. Perney and not some anybody else? That's why when the late Chad Delmonte had taken it upon himself to try to wipe out not just one but all three of her lifetime goals, he'd asked for trouble. Dorene had felt anger and a crazy, wild courage puff themselves up inside her chest like helium. She'd been giddy with it. Trouble is what Chad had been asking for, and trouble is what Dorene had plugged in and thrown into the bathtub with him. She'd slammed the door, watching herself as from a great distance away, connected only by a knot in her stomach. The knot was the size of the whole world as she'd known it.

Dorene had gone and grabbed a pillowcase from off the bed and thrown whichever of her things was handy into it, shaking head to toe, thinking about wolves—the big bad kind, like Chad was—and what huge, oh, pretty teeth they have when they smile at you. *All the better to eat you with, my dear.* Dorene had fled his apartment after going back to steal his wallet. She'd wandered in a blur, sleeping in people's backyards, trying to put together corners of lies Chad had told her with lies she'd told herself. Lies she'd slipped into as easily as putting on someone else's clothes in her size.

Dorene looked at her pink face drying in Buddy Whelper's bathroom mirror. She brushed her teeth with his toothbrush and, out of habit, her lips too—a Brooke Shields beauty tip to keep them soft and kissable. Dorene crept into Buddy's bedroom and paused at the sight of his bed bent double and him with it, folded in half, asleep. She got her pillowcase from beside his bed and tiptoed back to the bathroom. She dumped the contents onto the white tile floor. Dorene still couldn't believe it, but there it was. Everything she owned in a pile. If it wasn't so sad she'd laugh. She'd packed like a person on LSD, a crazy, out-of-her-mind person. If she ever needed to plead a case for temporary insanity when she'd killed Chad, all anyone had to do was look in that pillowcase to know she was certifiably nuts.

Dorene had to her name: a jar of Oil of Olay, battery-operated Godzilla slippers that roared with each step, four pairs of days of the week undies, an alarm clock, a permanently-blue mood ring and three stripping costumes besides the convict number she'd worn earlier. She had her choice. Dorene could start her new life dressed as Little Bo-peep, "Joan" Wayne (complete with toy gun, spurs and lasso) or Cat Woman. She felt tears well up but she bit them back and ran some cold water from the tap. She splashed the antacid off her face and, blurry though it was, made her choice to jingle jangle jingle.

FIVE

BUDDY called Cheryl. It was a thing he'd been doing in the middle of the night for some time now, even though mostly these nights Cheryl was sleeping beside a big man named Toomer Lester who had tattooed a pit bull over his heart. Cheryl confessed that once, in the heat of the moment, she'd licked and nibbled the pit bull's ears until a convulsive, joyful shiver had rocked her from head to toe. It was the best orgasm she'd ever had, and Buddy put that information at the back of his mind until he could figure out what to do with it. His instincts told him to get the topic back into waters he was safe swimming in, and he brought up plumbing and the nightmare of feminine hygiene products as clogging obstacles.

Whenever he called Cheryl it wasn't because he had a whole lot to say. He had some need to hear a woman's voice when he was in the dark, but also it relieved him to know there was a person out there who would put in her two cents on any given subject. Cheryl had no trouble with lengthy pauses either, and sometimes a lot of breathing went on before they hung up.

The phone Cheryl was an altogether different creature than his ex Cheryl. So much so that at first it had been mindboggling to Buddy. He'd grown accustomed to it, though, and now even pictured her differently, with her hair a windy pouf of curls, the way it would be if she ever stopped blow-drying it into sticks. Neither of them knew what had brought about the change in her, or whether relations between them might be any less strained if they were to get together again in person someday. Cheryl decided the pinpointable source of any amiable flux in her character was thanks to her beau, Toomer Lester, who had sparked to life the playful tiger of her innermost sexual being, and Buddy couldn't argue.

On the phone, Cheryl was bubbly and interesting and talked about issues that disturbed her—like clutter, high-impact aerobics, gun control, parallel parking. Gripes she wanted to air because in her opinion it was unhealthy to bottle poisons inside her "temple." It was the main way Buddy kept tuned in to society, since Cheryl's finger was pressing its pulse. She read every magazine she could subscribe to and watched or taped every talk show on the air, distilling for Buddy the gist, defining for him current trends and catchphrases. Words like *psycho-babble,* a term she was annoyed she hadn't come up with herself. Buddy knew about cocooning, being dysfunctional, codependent, post-feminist, whether or not a man should cry and for how long under what circumstances; he knew about the child within, and women who love too much. Cheryl reported that actually she was a news junkie, which meant she was addicted to CNN and world affairs. She was apt to comment, "I wonder what Saddam's up to now." She idolized all the TV anchormen but changed her mind frequently about who was smarter: Tom Brokaw or Peter Jennings. She saved a special place in her heart for Larry King. Buddy knew Cheryl's opinion on most matters. For her part, Cheryl seemed happy to have a willing ear at her disposal.

"Hi," Cheryl said, picking up on the first ring. "Toomer's drugged on 222s and snoring his way to dreamland. He chopped his finger off this morning and I had to find it and put it in a Baggie with ice cubes and carry it to the hospital, where they basically just nailed it on again. There's a big shiny nail head sticking out the top part of his finger, all black and bloody. They'll pull it out later when they figure the finger's going to stay put. A nurse told me she never saw one man who didn't scream like a baby when they pulled that big nail out of where it had grown used to being. Doctors have bigger arm muscles than drummers. She told me to excuse myself to the bathroom right before the event, since she's never seen a woman who didn't almost throw up standing by. Can you imagine how horrible it would be if you were the one person who actually did throw up, whether it was justified or not? They gave us a box of leeches to put on Toomer's finger—which I thought they were kidding about—to help stop the blood from clotting the wrong way. They weren't kidding, though, because Toomer rode home with the leeches on his lap, right where his chopped finger had been on the way there. Poor Toomer looked like he'd gotten a part in a horror movie he didn't know was casting. We were stopped at a traffic light and I turned to him and said, 'Toomer, baby, are you okay?' And he looked at me and then he laughed out loud, laughed and laughed, and then he was crying. Don't tell him I told you. But he was. Crying big tears and laughing at the same time and then he dozed off. About leeches: out of the five we put on today, three of them slithered away up his arm somewhere, leaving only two of them to get down to any serious sucking.

"So—surprise—I found another stash of Toomer's dirty magazines. Only they weren't *Hustler* or *Playboy* this time. I think Toomer listened to me when I told him those weren't real butts and noonies he was gawking at but air-brushed mutants. As I explained to him, 'Toomer, pubic hair does not grow in cute shapes, and besides, things are just too pink and pretty for my liking.' I don't think he'd ever thought about it that way and I know he was disappointed to hear it, but I said, 'You know what, Toomer, for a man your size you don't have a handle on anatomy.'

"So Toomer Lester went out and bought more magazines. Nudist colony magazines! I found them under the lawnmower in the garage—don't ask me how I thought to look there. There were these ordinary-looking men with slippers on, reading the newspaper with their penises lying on their legs like uncooked sausages. And speaking of food, their wives were in the kitchen cooking something nice for dinner, which they all planned to eat nude. They like to picnic. I noticed a lot of pictures of two couples and a dog sitting on the beach picnicking is why I know this. What else amazed me—if you looked just at their faces—nobody looked the way you'd expect when you saw their bodies. They were all fatter or skinnier than you'd expect them to be from the way they were dressed. Which told me something about barenaked people in general. They don't look like you think they will. Usually they look worse. With more body fat and hair and veins and moles than you imagined, kept hidden under their outfits.

"But what I mean about worse. Most women do not have perky breasts and dangerous S-curves. This was big news to me. I know about *The Beauty Myth*, but seeing a random sampling is believing and sweet relief! Those nudists were calm about letting it all hang out. Truly calm. I was so relieved to witness calm nakedness, to know it was possible, that I didn't think they looked worse or even ugly at all, which maybe I would have. But no. I loved those soft penises and sagging breasts. I drank them in like water in the desert. My heart was pounding with the discovery the way old Ponce de Leon's must have when he first kicked Florida. Before I knew it, I was pulling my panties down and lying on the cement floor of the garage, staring at those calm couples and feeling hot! hot! hot! Do you know what I mean, Buddy?"

"I can imagine." Buddy saw Cheryl, her cheek pressed to the dirty garage floor, giving herself what she wanted as simply as taking a drink when she was thirsty, and he felt proud of her. Desire was a hard, hurting memory.

"When Toomer's recuperated I want us to look at those pictures together, which he might find scintillating. I want us to waltz around in our slippers and picnic, the sun lighting up our flaws for the world to see. Ordinary flaws. Flaws that I've spent too much time worrying over. Now that I understand 'nobody's perfect' with my own eyes, I'm going to be naked every chance I get. Next time we speak, you can bet I'll be calm and naked. Of course, I will be wearing sunscreen, at least SPF 15, because of the stupid ozone mess we're in. I'm not sure where you stand on nudity these days, Buddy, but I hope you don't have much against it."

Buddy heard Cheryl breathing. He cleared his throat. "Well, there's a stripper in my bathroom," he said.

Buddy listened to Cheryl breathe more. His ex-mother-in-law had a hospital phobia and so she hadn't allowed doctors to remove her daughter's adenoids like they'd wanted to when Cheryl was a child, to correct her loud mouth-breathing and nasal speech. In movie theaters, in the quiet parts, people always turned around and glared at Cheryl like she could help it. "Excuse me for living" is what she always said, but Buddy knew it hurt her feelings. He heard her dip her hand into the bowl of sunflower seeds she kept by the phone, crack a shell between her teeth and spit it out.

"You have to repeat that, hon. I'm under the influence of a six-pack of blackberry wine coolers. I should clean the wax out of my ears. Now what did you say?"

Buddy cleared his throat again, more violently this time.

"You all right?" Cheryl asked.

"Fine," Buddy said. "A woman here took her clothes off to the tune of 'Tie a Yellow Ribbon 'Round the Ole Oak Tree' and now, as far as I know, she's in the bathroom." Buddy thought he heard Cheryl gasp. She loved gasping.

"Naked?" Cheryl said.

"There it is."

"In your bathroom! That's just what I've been talking about—I think I'm onto a trend." Cheryl breathed.

Her breathing was so even and low, so familiar after all in his ear, that Buddy found himself nodding off with the receiver cradled against his shoulder. "Cheryl?" he finally whispered.

"Wow!" she blasted back. "An exotic dancer! I wonder if she has breast implants. You'll know if you catch her massaging her titties. I read somewhere that the vast majority of exotic dancers have implants, which they see as the cost of doing business. There was a woman last week, on 'Geraldo,' I think, whose right tittie started moving around her entire body until it ended up in her armpit. She was considering having another implant put in where a boob should have been so her bras would fit again, but she didn't know. She didn't know about three titties and I can't blame her. What do you think of that? Of course there would only be the customary pair of nipples up front. Still. It would be a shame if your stripper's implants wandered, Buddy, because it put an end to that woman's career like you'd flicked off a switch or maybe she had cancer. Anyway, I better scoot. I promised Toomer I'd rent him a kung-fu movie from the all-night video for when he wakes up and remembers his finger is nailed on. He won't be thrilled to see the box of leeches on his bedside table, ready to suck his bloodclots either."

Buddy heard the click as Cheryl hung up. She always did that, never waiting for him to say good-bye and never saying it herself. Buddy was used to holding the receiver until the dial tone came on, which was fine because Cheryl left a kind of dial tone in his head anyway.

Buddy entered the kitchen to find Dorene burrowing in the fridge. What he saw of her mostly was rear, since she was wearing a jean skirt so short he could plainly see the top parting of her thighs and the initial out-swelling of her buttocks. On the kitchen table, he saw she'd loosened the plastic wrap from the plate of delicately scalloped potatoes and Lemon Chicken Divine he'd left out for her in case she woke up hungry, which it looked like she had. The meal had turned out better than he'd expected for a first attempt at a complex lemon cream sauce, and Buddy was pleased to allow that overall he was having fewer and fewer mishaps and eating less and less Chinese take-out from Wok & Roll at the last minute.

"Abby?" Buddy said, and on reflex she straightened up in the refrigerator.

"What!" Dorene turned, rubbing her head with the same hand that held a bottle of HP Sauce. She walked towards the kitchen table and with every step there was a deep electronic roar.

Buddy stared at the huge clawed slippers. What was it about women and slippers, he wondered. Cheryl had owned a rabbit-earred pair that she wore because she said they made her feel better. Better than what, he never knew. These monster ones had silver spurs attached to the heels somehow that Buddy guessed went with the cowgirl outfit and the lasso and pistol hanging from a tooled leather belt Dorene had slung around her hips. He squinted for a better look.

Dorene slumped down at the table and said, "I'm Joan Wayne. Cute, huh?" But the way she said it, in a plain flat voice, made Buddy think she didn't feel so cute or western.

He sat down across from her. She unscrewed the lid from the HP Sauce and thumped it on the bottom to make it come out directly above and onto the breast of lemon chicken. As the first blob of HP was making its way from the bottle, Buddy couldn't help but reach out his hand to protect the chicken, and so the sauce came out in a brown lump onto the back of his hand. Dorene raised her eyebrows at him coldly.

"Do you mind," she said, trying to push his hand out of the way with the still down-tilted bottle hovering over the chicken.

"Please," Buddy said, thwarting her nudges with defensive plays of his own. "You should at least try it first. It has a lemon cream sauce with just a dash of ginger, and a splash or two of sherry. Aunt Cindy's Lemon Chicken Divine is what the recipe's called."

"Who are you supposed to be, the Galloping Gourmet?" Dorene jabbed the bottle down on the back of Buddy's knuckles and he pulled his hand away at the pain. Dorene went ahead and poured HP over the chicken breast, and as an afterthought over the scalloped potatoes too. "There," she said spitefully, "that looks yummy." After a few bites she seemed to soften. "I must be starving. This is delicious."

"Thank you very much," Buddy said. "I'm cooking my way through the poultry chapter." They sat in silence while Dorene ate. Buddy had a thing about polite table manners. Dorene had a nice way of chewing, he noticed. Because Cheryl couldn't breathe through her nose, she'd had to eat with her mouth slightly open. A lot could be learned about a person, Buddy thought, judging by how fast or how slow they chewed each morsel. Dorene had a brisk pace to her forkfuls but her chewing still managed to appear delicate and thorough. She swallowed invisibly.

"So, Whelper, you live alone here?" Dorene wiped her mouth, with a mind to going back to the fridge for dessert. A piece of coconut pie or a brownie, if she could find them, would be perfect. "I don't see even a trace of a little pet. Don't you like animals? I believe in kindness towards strays. Charity starts at home. Well, you know that. Hugging a pooch is supposed to be soul medicine."

"Even small dogs are not their best in apartments," Buddy said. "My mother had a hairless Mexican dog who tried jumping off her second-floor balcony five or six times, injuring himself slightly every time. She got tired of vet bills and bought him a special collar and leash which enabled him to jump from the railing without falling to the ground, since it was the landings that were taking their toll. Every day now, when she comes home from work, there's Pedro swinging two floors up, kicking his legs and running in the air like he's trying to make it back to Mexico. 'Pedro,' my mother says, 'I see you're doing your exercises again, baby muscle man.' And she pulls him inside and gives him real beef in a tiny majolica bowl."

"That's a Chihuahua, right? Those don't count. Those aren't dogs—they're something else. Martians." Dorene had gone to the fridge, roaring all the way, in search of dessert.

"Pedro is not a Martian, although his life is not easy. I know how it is when even failed escape attempts become necessary. I can't speak for Pedro, but adultery provided some relief."

"Is that right?" Dorene said. "You think Pedro's got a girlfriend?" She brought out a pie-like dessert with red filling and lacy dribbles of chocolate across the top. "What's this?" she said.

"Raspberry Angel Meringue Tart," Buddy answered, helpless to keep the pride from his voice. "The recipe called for a teaspoon of cream of tartar, which was a surprise."

"So—" Dorene said, her hands on her hips, "where's the Cool Whip? I have a sweet tooth."

SIX

DORENE faked being asleep when the phone rang first thing in the morning. She could hear Buddy moving around, getting dressed while he talked, calming somebody down about a rock that had broken a window inches from a baby's crib.

"Listen," Buddy said, "you have no idea how many fatal accidents happen at home. The police don't want it getting out for fear of mass hysteria. Poisonings are common as fruitflies. Life, on the whole, is a game of dodgeball. I'll be there in a jiffy."

Dorene tried snoring in a way she hoped wasn't phony, shifting her eyes back and forth under her lids as though she was in the middle of a racy dream, in case Buddy was looking. She kept this up the entire time he was getting tools down from the living-room wall, next to where she was curled in the La-Z-Boy with a cozy afghan over her. Just before he shuffled out the door, Dorene peeked and saw him adjust a pair of wide plastic goggles and pull on a hardhat with a flashlight up front. "Christ," she said under her breath as the door banged closed.

She knew Buddy assumed she would let herself out and be gone by the time he got back, since they'd already said their goodbyes in the middle of the night, after finishing off the pie. "Nice to meet you," Buddy had said, and Dorene had felt a stab of guilt. She'd always been an empathetic person, someone who didn't like to impose. She steadfastly rooted for underdogs and felt sorry for Buddy being so polite and hospitable when he was about to gain an unwanted roommate and, probably, be questioned by the police for harboring a criminal. Being an accessory after the fact.

Dorene climbed into Buddy's bed. It was still warm, with the sheets loose and soft from him sleeping in them. She pressed the control switches, trying things until her head was lying flat but her legs were raised up in the air. She shut her eyes. She saw Chad and his Don Johnson pretty-boy smile. She let herself sing "Sweet Dreams" by Patsy Cline, who, like herself, knew about loving the man you hated. She hugged Buddy's pillow and tried to stop the panic that was rising inside her. She didn't know what else to do.

The way she saw it, after you killed someone, you had to hide, or even better, you had to *disappear*. And since the police would naturally check your connections first—friends, relatives, places you liked to hang out—the best way to disappear was to move in with a complete and total stranger. A "B. Whelper." Provided that person kept quiet, you'd be safe indefinitely. As long as you never went out anywhere or did anything you used to love doing. Like watching your favorite bands perform or browsing through used-record stores. Dorene began to cry. She toyed with the bed switches until she got the top part moving up and down, which felt almost as if someone was rocking her.

Over the past few days, she'd run the gamut of emotions. Why hadn't she just left Chad like any normal person would have instead of doing a Dirty Harry revenge number on him and ruining her life in the bargain? She was too proud and mean when it came to her dreams. Her dreams were fires. They burned in her like J.F.K.'s memorial flame and were that hard to put out.

Still, it was Chad's fault for even trying. He'd set the wheels of his own demise in motion and it served him right. He'd lied and cheated and hurt her so badly she'd wanted to die. She'd wanted to die the way old animals go under a chair, tuck down and decide that's enough. For a while Chad had made her forget that Dorene LaTisha Perney was going to make something of herself. When she sang, people were going to understand things that maybe they couldn't put into words but they would feel by the way she moved her voice—and her hips. Big, important things. The music would comfort and change them. *Do-wop*, she'd sing, and men would start paying child support. *Ooh ooh, Ba-by* and men would scrub floors; others would think to take home flowers and honey their tongues. Chad had made her forget that she was a fighter, and it took all her strength and a bunch of inner pep talks to remind her. Nobody was going to treat her the way he treated her and get away with it. A million-dollar smile and some heavenly choir-song foreplay did not exempt him from having to be a decent human being.

The problem now was how did she intend to make her dreams come true hiding out in Buddy Whelper's bachelor pad? Dorene looked around the blank box of a room. She sniffed and wiped her nose on the suede fringe on the arm of her cowboy shirt. For starters she had to stop feeling sorry for herself. Destinee said people made their own beds. "Damn straight," Dorene thought out loud, her breath catching in jags from crying so hard. There was still fight in her, and if she had to take on Buddy Whelper she would. Her next move was to persuade him to let her stay in his apartment indefinitely, or at least until the coast was clear, but she had no idea how she might do that. Money, maybe, if she could get some from Destinee to pay him off. One thing she did know was she'd better keep him away from the news and "America's Most Wanted." When everything blew over, she could worry about just how she aimed to become a famous backup singer, get married and have cute twins without ending up behind bars.

Dorene fixed herself a coffee. She smoked her last cigarette and became, officially, a nonsmoker—an easier move than it would seem later, she knew. She snuck around the apartment, opening and closing drawers, cupboards, closets, snooping for entertainment, although it barely rated. There wasn't much but she got a sneaky thrill. In the hall closet, shelves had been fitted to hold cans of paint. There were dozens of cans, all sizes and different colors. Dorene's eye was drawn to a small can of lilac enamel. She took it out of the closet and toured the apartment anew, scrutinizing it now with a decorator's gaze, looking for something that would be cheered by a touch of lilac. Her sight came to rest on Buddy's tools hanging on the living-room wall. Dull, drab, black handles. Dorene pried open the lid and one by one dipped the handles into the pretty paint. She held each of the tools until they'd quit dripping, then carefully replaced them in their racks. She was charmed by how much softer the entire room became when accented with lavender, the tools hardly looking like tools at all anymore, and she felt a blush of satisfaction.

By the time she heard Buddy's key in the lock some while later, Dorene was Little Bo-peep and restless. There wasn't a whole hell of a lot to do in his cramped quarters. She'd put her stripping tape on in the ghetto blaster and was singing to Rickie Lee Jones's moody version of "My Funny Valentine." She was rowing as fast as she could on Buddy's rowing machine, imagining Chad chasing up behind her in a speeding boat of his own.

SEVEN

BUDDY had been feeling peculiar all morning and when he saw Dorene on the rowing machine, singing and gazing out the window at the chestnut tree, he knew why. His adored privacy had been sundered to make room for this person who seemed no longer to be a cowgirl but some kind of Heidi. He thought she would've gone by now. He still wasn't sure why she'd been there in the first place.

"Hey," Dorene said, easing speed.

"I forgot a screwdriver," Buddy said, crossing to the wall.

"Uh-oh." Dorene's eyes darted ahead of him. "Your timing's bad. They're still tacky."

"Uhhh," Buddy said when he saw his tools, as if he'd had the wind kicked out of him.

"Pardon?"

"You—"

"Now you won't get them mixed up with anyone else's. You'll always know which are yours. Like a signature. Industrial art."

"But— The grips were leather."

"What's your point?"

"You don't paint leather."

"Who passed that law? I think they look neat. Lilac is an easy color to live with. A poignant color. You'll get used to it. You're just in shock. Shock plays all kinds of mean tricks on a body and spirit. There was a teeny second when I thought I'd made a mistake but it passed."

Buddy banged out, minus his tools and peace of mind, slumped down the third-floor corridor like his feet were made of lead. He really didn't know why the stripper was still in his apartment. He should have asked her. Why are you here? Would you mind getting out now and leave me be? He had to learn to seize the moment, shoot off his mouth and regret it later if he had to. It bugged him to think of her on his rowing machine. Worse was the sense that he'd made a fundamental, costly mistake by not escorting her out the door last night, whether she was able-bodied enough to walk through it or needed his help. That would have been the smart thing to do—any fool would have done that. It wasn't right for a woman to expect to knock on a stranger's door, peel off her clothes and then stay the night, plus hang around all the next day too. Not to mention that he was the *wrong* stranger, his identity mistaken, she had the wrong address. How many B. Whelpers could there be in Savannah, Georgia? Buddy tried to tell himself he was fretting for nothing, she'd probably left on his heels. If only, he thought. If only he'd thrown her out politely but firmly when he had the chance, he wouldn't have worked himself into such a state. Besides, what did he know about her, this Rene, Dorene, Abigail, Abby? For all the information he had, she could be a professional thief who was stealing his worldly possessions that instant. Not that he had a whole lot worth taking—his television, his tools. Buddy gritted his teeth. His *pink* tools. Well, she was welcome to them. He stopped and turned in his tracks, intending to pluck her from his apartment a.s.a.p. while he had more than reasonable doubt and just cause.

Mrs. Feeny, an eighty-year-old tenant, stepped into the hallway directly in front of him and blew a silver whistle. "Watch this," she said, twirling a shining baton that flashed in the light.

She flung the chrome bar into the air and caught it still spinning, ducked it under a bent knee. "Pretty good for a senior. I've been looking for you, mister." She prodded Buddy's chest with a bony knuckle. "We've got a problem." She shuffled her blown-out flip-flops into her apartment, her gray head lowered into the V of her bathrobe. Buddy followed.

"First the doctors drug me so I can't operate my own bowels. Now my dreams are being interrupted." Mrs. Feeny grabbed hold of Buddy's sleeve and twisted. "You don't appreciate a thing until it's wrecked. No one does. My bowels are only one example. I used to be regular as the Fourth of July. Hal said you could set your watch by my poop in the morning, like it was Greenwich Mean Time. Poor Hal was constipated practically his entire life because of an inability he had to digest lactose. He was tortured by his intestines. He told me he pictured vicious snakes inside him. Live with that, I dare you. We kept a transistor radio in the bathroom to drown out the grunts he made when he was trying to go. You can bet he envied me my five minutes in and out, with no straining whatsoever, easy as pudding. Not like now. These days I use the radio myself more often than not. Everything in me is turning hard as walnuts."

Mrs. Feeny batted her eyes at Buddy, which he hoped was her usual way of blinking and not any kind of flirtation. He gently removed her little hand from his sleeve. "What do you need me to fix, Mrs. Feeny?" Buddy let her see him glance at his watch.

"Nobody has time to shoot the breeze with old people. When you've finally got something to say, nobody wants to hear it. Nobody gives a fig about old people who're all on death row. Senior citizens may as well cut out their tongues for all the use they are. Cut them out and throw them in the trash compactor. My problem's in the bedroom."

Mrs. Feeny led Buddy through cluttered rooms of ornate, overstuffed furniture into her bedroom, which was painted midnight blue with white trim. A small TV was switched on to a talk show. The screen was a close-up of a grim teenager with her head shaved. Beneath her flashed the words "Hates Everybody and Everything."

Mrs. Feeny clucked her tongue. "Imagine. Somebody ought to take that girl into a field and shoot her in the kneecaps. Nobody can hate everything. It's impossible. There are some very nice things—monkeys and fountains. Peanut brittle. I know from experience living with Hal, who hated *almost* everybody and everything, that it's possible to hate just about everything. But at least Hal was reasonable enough to leave himself some room to like the odd thing if he wanted to. Me, for example. Hal liked me. Every Valentine's Day he bought me a spoon for my collection. And that's not all. We took milk baths together like movie stars for forty years. What do you think of that?"

"Sounds nice."

"You're right, it was. Hal could be a pain in the neck, though. What about you, Mr. Whelper? Do you have a sweetheart? You can't expect to be a hermit living in an apartment building. There's something warped about you. Those goggles. And I'm practically blind from that high beam on your hat. What's the idea, anyway—who are you trying to be? You want to be anonymous, another face in the crowd nobody will notice? But it's not that easy. It's not easy to lose yourself in a crowd. It takes talent to get to be left alone, and it costs. You have to be sure you want it. Either you do or you don't. Anyway, you just can't be a hermit in an apartment building. You're an *anti*-hermit. Clean up and take that plump lady, Rhoda, to a movie. She has lonely stamped all over her. But don't tell her she looks lonely whatever you do or she'll bite your head off. 'I'm not miserable. Hear me, I'm not miserable,' she kept saying. But she is. Miserable as a hound. Treat or go dutch, I could care less, that part's up to you."

"Mrs. Feeny, is there something you want me to fix? I don't see anything broken in here." Buddy turned, his light bouncing off the walls, skipping over the furniture.

Mrs. Feeny knocked on his hardhat. "Let's hope your head's not as thick as this helmet." She pointed to a stormy seascape hanging on a wall. Buddy shone his light on it. "That wall is like tissue paper. I can hear everything going on next door through it. I want you to add some padding. Make it soundproof so I can sleep." She lowered her voice to a hoarse whisper. "Those people enjoy adult games, porno videos. They are reminding me about S-E-X, to spell it out for you. A lot of us seniors are forced to live like nuns against our wills, against our better judgment." Mrs. Feeny pounded on her chest dramatically. "I'm in here, in this pruny old body, perfect as ever. I'm not any different than when I was sixteen. Just you wait and see if *you* don't wither like a flower for lack of sun. Nobody wants to water my roots anymore."

Buddy stacked some sofa pillows against Mrs. Feeny's bedroom wall and secured them with electrical tape, then he took the stairs back down to his own apartment. There was no sign of Dorene when he first went inside, but before he could relax, he heard the toilet flush. Dorene came out of the bathroom and jumped when she saw him standing there like he was the one in the way, out of place.

"God, you scared me. What are you doing back so soon?"

On the breeze from the open window came the scent of her, light and fragrant, and Buddy sank into the La-Z-Boy. He was spooked. He couldn't shake the notion that some kind of feminine spell was being cast on him. Tiny muscles around his mouth began to twitch.

"You don't look so hot," Dorene said. "I better get you a nice Dr Pepper," and she went to the kitchen, feeling his dazed eyes on her back. Maybe they'd start out taking turns fainting on each other, because that's exactly what Buddy looked like he was about to do. She'd been through it often enough lately to know.

Buddy couldn't think, couldn't fathom, why Dorene's dresses were so short, her tops so undone. Didn't she have to be somewhere? He took the glass she offered him, spilling some soda on his shirt in the process. He looked down at the spreading mark, darkening as though it were a cloud moving over his heart or blood from a direct gunshot.

Dorene smiled at him. She gently took off his goggles and hardhat and put her palm on his forehead to check for fever.

The hand felt remarkably cool to Buddy, soft, tender on his brow, and he closed his eyes, allowing his head to press into it the way it wanted to.

Dorene thought Buddy probably did have a fever and at the moment she was about to tell him he was burning up his eyes opened and he looked at her. It was startling. The look was clear and trusting, almost grateful. A baby's look in a sweet moment. Dorene had never seen a man look like that before, but then maybe that was her fault for paying so much attention to teeth. Buddy's teeth were nothing special, she'd already noted. Teeth did not have it in them to reflect moods, or speak words you could almost hear; they weren't windows to souls or anything like eyes were. Which, come to think of it, was probably why Dorene stuck with them.

"Abby?"

"Yes, Whelper?"

"Are you Heidi now?"

"Little Bo-peep."

"Little Bo-peep who lost her sheep and didn't know where to find them." Buddy was spellridden and befogged. He'd come unanchored, drifted away from his home shore and all he could do was circle and wait. Wait to reclaim his rightful space, sheltered, insulated from storms and nature's frenzies.

"I guess you're wondering what I'm still doing here." Dorene tugged at the hem of her frilly dress and sighed.

Her eyes were brimming with tears, and Buddy knew she thought there was something he could do about it. Something she wanted him to do about it. He was drowning. He was going down down down, sinking low. He was standing in his underpants in front of his wife, Cheryl, being drunk and only himself. It was important. Be true.

"Whelper?"

"What?"

"I guess I've had kind of a checkered past. I'm a Catholic. I feel this real need to confess. Please would you come into the bathroom with me?" Dorene took Buddy's glass from him, drank the rest of the Dr Pepper and set it down on the floor. "Come on," she said, prying him out of his easy chair. "Sit there," she told him, indicating the toilet, while she climbed into the bathtub and pulled closed the shower curtain. "Okay," she said. "This'll do."

EIGHT

BUDDY put his head in his hands. He saw the toddler from that morning eating pieces of banana in his high chair. The rock that had broken the window was lying on the carpet where it had landed, not even a foot from where the child had been dreaming in his crib. Shards of glass glinted around it. The mother kept going over to her baby, saying "Precious, my precious" in his ear while she kissed his hair and nuzzled him with her cheek. The baby had his mouth full of banana. It wasn't until Buddy had finished taping the window and was about to leave that the woman picked the boy up and Buddy saw that he had only one leg, the stump of the other came out just past his diaper. The woman lifted her child into the air. "Don't you think he's adorable?" she said. "To me, he is a pleasant thrill. There is nothing I resent doing for him." The boy had grinned, and when he did, a silvery line of drool spun from his lip like a web. Watching it, the mother said, "My son doesn't know yet that he is any less than others. I try to be brave but I don't know how much more of this I can stand. A rock, of all things, plain as a bully on the nursery floor." The boy narrowed his eyes, lunged for Buddy's hardhat and with his hand snuffed the single ray of light.

"Whelper," Dorene said from behind the shower curtain, "can you see me?"

"Just the shape of you. I know you're standing up."

"I believe I'll go ahead and confess then. I was going to tell lie upon lie, a whole pack of lies, but you seem like a nice man and now I don't want to. I like your cooking and that hospital bed of yours, this gleaming white bathroom. The truth is supposed to set you free, though of course it doesn't. Oh shit, Whelper, I'm in a heap of trouble. My name's not Abby or some of those others we talked about. It's Dorene. Dorene LaTisha Perney." Dorene began to cry at the sound of her own name, which suddenly seemed so unextraordinary, the name of a person destined for nothing great. "I'm a murderer is what it boils down to. I need to hide out with a stranger for a while. You. I can get money. I can pay you for it."

"A murderer?" Buddy said. "Hide out. But. Why me?"

"I don't know. I know it's not fair." Dorene stuck her arm out from behind the curtain and waggled her fingers. "Tissue," she said. Buddy tore some toilet paper from the roll and put a wad in her hand. "As something to think about, Kleenex now has baby lotion in it, if you want to consider softness next time you shop. Why you? Honestly, I don't know. In some ways, I feel sorry Fate bull's-eyed you and not the next anybody down the road." Dorene dropped the used toilet paper on the floor.

"I picked a strange part of town, a strange building, a strange name from the list of names on the mailboxes. B. Whelper. I knocked on your door and you opened it. I came inside and stripped. I thought that would be bonding and besides it would be harder for you to kick me out if I was naked. Anyway, stripping is mostly what I've been doing lately, thanks to Chad. He's the one I killed. Chad Delmonte, my dead fiancé. It even rhymes, like a nursery song. He told me stripping was a tried-and-true way to break into show business. You overcome butterflies and get used to thinking of your body as an unshy instrument. Chad was the 'agency' I mentioned earlier. Mostly it was stag parties I was stripping at. Chad seemed to have dozens of stag friends who preferred to pay him directly. You know what? I never spotted one groom-to-be the whole time, not one man who looked like he was ready to honor and cherish. I wasn't any closer to being a backup singer than I was to the moon. But I didn't know that. I was too busy getting naked in rooms full of smelly men, being pawed and hooted at. I can tell you this: when you commit a crime of passion, which mine was, you are so close to killing yourself that you have to kill the other person in order to save your own skin. It's you or them. Self-defense is not a lame excuse." Dorene paused.

"And you are so in love, Whelper. You dream about having your name in silver letters next to theirs on a cocktail napkin. You dream about it even during the day when you're out doing interesting things that have nothing to do with getting married. Chad said he could see living with me until he was pushing up daisies. Which I held him to, I guess. He didn't mean it. I had these special engraved invitations printed on fancy white paper. Wedding invitations. I was thrilled that I could read the writing with my eyes closed, letting my finger trace over the words like I was blind. I was blind. Chad made me get them printed leaving a blank space for the date—he said I could fill it in later using a ballpoint pen when he let me know. When you are an eyelash away from being happy, you find a reason to look the other way. You turn the other cheek so that one can get smashed too."

Dorene took off her clothes and threw them onto the tile floor, then she turned the water on, hot enough to steam. Buddy watched through the thin fabric curtain as she tilted her head back into the flow. He felt the heat spread across his own scalp, down the back of his neck, the small of his back on down, lower. It was like watching a movie that hadn't come into focus yet. It made him edgy and excited. Achy for things to be clear.

"Near the end," Dorene said softly and Buddy leaned closer, "we were making love less and less, and when we did it was always from behind. That says something sad to a woman."

Buddy stood. He saw himself in the fogged mirror as he unbuttoned his shirt. He had a farmer's tan, with a white chest and white arms down to the elbow, dark face and neck. His hair hit his collarbone. He took off his pants. He pulled the shower curtain back and stepped into the tub, facing Dorene. The water was pouring over her. She looked at him, naked, not an arm's length away, and he thought there was a little bit of a smile in the look. Dorene gazed down the length of him and he stood for it, shifting his weight, aware of his semi-hard cock. She shook her head and made a small sound in her throat. Then she reached for his hand and brought it up to her mouth, kissed the back of it and held it against her cheek. A tear slid from her eye and crossed his knuckle.

Buddy took the soap from the shelf and smoothed it over Dorene's shoulders, her breasts, stomach, hips, thighs, turning her this way and that as he needed to, like a doll or himself he was washing. He didn't take advantage. They were walking on glass, everyone was. You went through the world stepping as lightly as you could, trying not to get cut, hoping for something somewhere worth the effort, worth believing.

When he'd finished soaping her, he moved Dorene under the pulse of water. "You're sparkling," he said, "clean." But she didn't hear. Her eyes were shut, her head held back and Buddy bet she was wondering to herself, what next. How you can't guess what next.

NINE

DORENE was stretched out on Buddy's bed watching a dating game show on his television set, which was all her attention span could handle. She was dying for a cigarette. Buddy was in the kitchen whipping up Teriyaki Chicken Wings for their dinner. He'd been kind in the shower, considerate and gentle when he touched her. They hadn't made love.

On the TV program, the women were called ladies and they all had big hair and ultra-bright smiles, slanted legs crossed at the ankles, voices they tried their best to make sexy. The men were disappointments with necklaces and wore white athletic socks with black shoes. The reason Dorene watched, what she waited for, was the moment after all the stupid questions had been asked and the come-ons purred, when the man (Bachelor Number Whatever) stepped out from behind a partition and the woman who had picked him got to take a hard look at who she thought was Mr. Right. Dorene liked to see the mean letdown, the fizzled expectation leap like static, almost visibly, in the space between them before the woman would decide she'd be a good sport and blink closed her eyes while the man pecked her tight lips like an aunt's. Dorene knew about that moment. The hope-charged "pleases" suddenly muffled, although up until then they'd been said like prayers, silently. Chanted over and over—*please*—with hardly any actual thought but oh, urgency. Desire. *Please.*

Dorene knew what it was to set your own booby traps and make yourself smile as you tripped and fell into the hole you'd dug for yourself. The last one to see a thing for what it was, a diamond from a dud, a spade for a spade and call it. She knew the all-the-time, everywhere audience went ahead and cheered any choice you made because they weren't you and—what did they know—maybe you'd manage to turn things around, get happy? Maybe you'd surprise the world and everybody in it who was still saying please please please. Even if they didn't know they were or why they were asking so nicely. *Please,* everyone said. *Pretty please.*

Dorene had told Buddy everything. She hadn't planned to, but the words had come rolling out of her mouth like gumballs. She'd had her head on his chest as they'd lain side by side, barenaked in his up-folded bed. There was a restorative tonic to simply holding another solid, living person close. It took Dorene by surprise when she suddenly felt so drawn to Buddy that she wanted to jump on top of him. She'd never been with a man who was as ragged and rough-looking as he was; her boyfriends had all been routinely handsome. But the truth also was, she'd never had a man she felt as comfortable being around. Despite his woolly appearance, there was something about Buddy that appealed to her. She couldn't take her eyes off him. She loved the lines around his mouth. He was strange and awkward, no doubt, but there was a simple, perfect grace about him, too. His body was lean and sinewy, skeletal almost, the hard bones of his frame visible just beneath his flesh. His right ankle and foot were badly misshapen, the toes mashed together, one atop the other, in a way that looked clumsy and sore. A pink scar ran from his ankle to the jut of his hip. A *Playgirl* centerfold he wasn't, but still Dorene was entirely thankful for the fact of him lying beside her.

She'd gone ahead and told him the messy pages of her autobiography, pages she wished she could just Wite-Out and rewrite.

She'd told Buddy things about her childhood and living with Destinee's remarkable ears. Ears that, just when Dorene wanted to be heard the most and taken seriously, went deaf to her. There were people Dorene had sat beside on a bus that she felt she knew better than her mother. That was the peculiar thing about strangers and family—your heart told you one thing but the reality of the relationships was another. In a short life, it seemed a shame you didn't have more control over your blood. There were nice things Dorene remembered: the safety of Destinee's hand holding hers while they crossed the road, her firm grip. But she was never just right for her mother as she was. Destinee was always making excuses for her in public to explain away her shyness or lack of gentility towards her mother's newest heartthrob. Dorene was never in the mood Destinee expected her to be in. And vice versa. Their whole relationship was a near miss, wild arrows shot from Cupid's shifty bow.

Unlike Buddy, Dorene felt lighter, unburdened with the telling. She took her heavy load and dumped it gratefully on Buddy's knobby shoulders.

"A few days ago," she'd begun, "I was a free agent. I could do pretty much anything I wanted. Think of the things you like to do and then forget about doing them. Forget about seeing a movie or buying tickets to a concert. Now I have to hide out, cooped up like a bug in a jar because a two-timing, pretty-boy ratshit named Chad Delmonte thought he could treat me any damned way he wanted. As if I didn't count for anything. As if it didn't matter if I was ever a backup singer or the mother of cute twins. Well, I showed him, didn't I? You don't mess with Dorene LaTisha Perney and get away with it. He looked like the sorriest son of a bitch you'd ever want to see, lying in that bathtub with the blow-dryer shooting hot air between his legs. Frying his balls off."

"What?" Buddy had said. "You lost me. You electrocuted someone?" And he'd asked one question after another, so confused that Dorene had to keep going over the whole thing from top to bottom while his eyes got rounder and wilder like he was trying to find the door out of a dark room.

She'd told Buddy about getting pregnant some night of many when Chad had rolled her onto her stomach so that he wouldn't have to look at her face. Those nights he'd pulled her hips up in the air with one hand and pinched her nipples with the other. Foreplay and Chad were oil and water. Always there was the pillowcase between her teeth, dry as skin.

A shiver of a smile, a wince, had crossed Chad's face when she'd told him she was pregnant, and then he'd pressed his fingers into his temples, hard white pressure.

"Chad?" she'd said. "I'm scared too. But there's ample chance it's our twins coming along. Nature knows what it's doing." She'd gone to him and curved against him, fitted herself as best she could to him, and breathed in his after-shave. She actually felt like the "Natural Woman" Aretha sang about; she was proud her body worked the way it was intended to. *You make me feel,* the song went. *When my heart was in the lost and found, you came along to claim it.* Chad had touched her cheek lightly with his fingertips before slapping her face with his open hand. He'd caught her as she reeled backward, gripped her shoulders to hold her steady while he drove his knee into her stomach. On the ground, Dorene had clung to the skinny legs of the coffee table and tried to pull herself up. Chad had kicked her ribs, kicked anywhere he could make contact, until she'd passed out finally, tasting blood.

Hours later, Chad was on a date and she was in the Emergency, telling a doctor how she'd fallen down some stairs. It was as if she'd been sleeping with her eyes open and now she'd woken up and was trying to figure out how she'd gotten to be where she was at. She didn't care about the doctor examining her, she was taking her own inventory. Nothing felt broken exactly, although there were major parts of her that felt pulpy and too heavy to move, something crackled in her chest when she breathed, and if she twisted at all, stabs of pain knifed her ribs. The doctor had given her a sanitary pad to hold between her legs. Her twin babies were gone. Their names, had she been able to speak them, would have been petals on her lips, blossoms, delicate and fully flowered.

What wasn't gone, though—in fact what she had found—was the essential Dorene LaTisha Perney. A woman with unplumbed depths, worthy of marvel. True, she was a latecomer to seeing life and love minus the rosy filter. And true, being dead outright instead of only stomped to within an inch of her life would have hurt a whole lot less than what she was suffering. But still, despite the pain, there was within her the unmistakable electric tingle of bravery surging through her veins, firing her up, ready to fight. Ever since childhood, it was a feeling that had come upon her every now and then, like it or not, wanted or not, a mix of cool stubbornness and red-hot bravery that usually made whatever trouble she was in worse.

Though her bruises had healed on the outside, sooner than she'd have thought, it wasn't the same for her inside. Dorene had woken up one morning, eaten breakfast alone—unlike Chad, who hadn't been home all night—and then bought a newspaper, meaning to study her horoscope to see if anything good might be expected to happen anytime soon. If so, she would wait for it and devote herself to doing the crossword puzzle. If not, she'd nix him.

"I know it doesn't seem right or make much sense, Whelper, not to me either, but at the time it was simple."

After reading the little horoscope two or three times, Dorene had accepted that no insight or advice was forthcoming, for or against, nothing remotely useful whatsoever was hidden beneath the words, so she'd might as well give up scratching to uncover it. Nobody was going to talk her out of snuffing Chad Delmonte if that's what she had a mind to do.

She used a pair of nail scissors to strip the electrical cord on her hair dryer. Then she waited for Chad to come back from his date. "After a while, I got thinking I should kill myself instead. I might have too, except luckily for me, Chad came in with a love-bite the size of Atlanta on his neck. It was the icing on top of all the hate I'd been feeling. I just knew then, and one part of me moved out of the way so the other part could take over. My personality split in two: good and bad, simple as that.

"I poured a bath and convinced Chad to get in, acting as though it was all going to lead to something, which it was, but not to the sexy wrestle he had in mind. When he was laid back in the water, I turned the hair dryer on and dropped it in the tub between his legs. Water splashed up into my eyes. I was blind, listening to this awful hissing coming from the tub. When I opened my eyes, the ceiling lights were strobing on and off. That scared me more than anything. I'd see Chad for a split second and then I wouldn't. I bolted for the door, slipped on the wet tiles, scrambled on my hands and knees to get out. I just wanted to get out the door. I heard sobbing and realized it was my own. That was strange. I heard it more than I felt it. I kept imagining Chad rising from the water to come after me, mad as he'd ever been. Mad as hell."

Buddy had gone as chalky as the Tums he'd begun to swallow by the mouthful.

"You know," Dorene went on, tugging at a springy hair around Buddy's nipple, "this was supposed to be my freewheeling new life. I really thought, presto, I'd become a famous backup singer without Chad standing in my way, beating me up and wrecking all my plans. I thought the sky was the limit in the career-option department. I could be anything I wanted to be. Everything I aspired to. Well, the joke's on me. I can't even go outside. I can't buy a new dress to upgrade my wardrobe from a stripper's. I can't do anything but sit here and become anonymous. And I keep wondering if I didn't let Chad hurt me. If somewhere deep down I wasn't asking for it. I know that's not the right thing to say but maybe, when I said no, I didn't mean it. What was I offering him? Love? Sex, rape, sometimes the line between them wasn't all that clear to me. It could be damn hard, chomping that pillow sometimes, to tell which was which."

Dorene rubbed the palms of her hands up and down her arms, and shivered. "But that's crazy, isn't it, Whelper? That's crap! The son of a bitch killed my babies and nearly me too, for all he cared. I didn't deserve that. Not for wanting love. Ha. Love. For that little while I was pregnant, I had all the reasons anyone could need, or ask, for dancing on with this life. Simple things too beautiful to cost a thing. The way, in the morning, the sun edges the drawn shade with gold. My eyes were getting presents wherever I looked. The world was my oyster and I was its pearl. Well, that's a laugh."

Dorene turned her face into the crook of Buddy's arm. He didn't know what to make of any of it. He searched in vain for something to say that might absolve her. He patted her hair helplessly, awed by its softness.

"I don't know," he told her truthfully.

"What don't you know? If you mean whether I can stay here or not, you don't have a choice. I'll try not to take up too much room, or get under your feet, but I'm staying put until I can figure out how in hell I'm going to step back into the world without doing time." Dorene's chin crinkled bitterly and she rubbed each eye with a single angry swipe. "God, I'm so tired. If only I could go to sleep and wake up in someone else's life. You know, I'm tired enough that it seems like it might be possible. If I could just sleep."

"Everything will turn out the way it's supposed to," Buddy told her. "You'll see."

"Is that intended to make me feel better? Because it doesn't. How would you know about things turning out the way they're supposed to? Unless I'm mistaken, you haven't killed anybody. You're not a first-degree murderer, are you? You're not supposed to be in jail right now, which is where I'm supposed to be if we're talking about consequences, Mr. Cold Comfort. I am not moving."

"Okay," Buddy said.

"What?" Dorene said. "You mean it?"

Buddy shrugged. He'd gone too far to turn back.

The look Dorene flashed him was long, overlong he felt, and rimmed with curiosity that turned to fondness. It was a shimmery look that lit her face from within and that, despite everything, he couldn't help gladdening at. The kiss she gave his stubbled cheek was light and swift as a child's, there and gone so fast he hardly felt it.

"Sorry I was grumpy. Chad Delmonte ran a good race in the looks category, but what you are is a prince hiding inside a beast, no offense. I've always loved that fairy tale about hidden beauty. Somewhere in the world I believe there is a treasure chest of love and luck just waiting for me to find. It could be you're the map of my dreams."

Buddy lay on the bed after Dorene fell asleep, flexing the toes of his good foot up and down sporadically. He was trying to think into words what was bothering him, but he couldn't manage it. His mind drifted from thought to thought, all of them slightly blurry. What he suspected was his common sense was being eroded, emotion was plundering his logic. He began to feel that he might forget everything about himself—who he'd been and what he was. If he wasn't careful, he would forget that he had lived alone without a twinge of loneliness.

As a kid, he'd gone hunting. It wasn't something Buddy was proud to recall, but it came to him. He'd aimed his BB gun at a young rabbit, shot and shot, until the creature was so pumped full of pellets it couldn't run. Buddy had watched the rabbit drag itself away on its belly. He thought about willpower, that staggering determination to beat the odds against escape. The wondrous weight of a gut full of lead and the crystal sense to know it.

TEN

THERE WAS SOMETHING about bowling that appealed to Buddy, and he gave a loud hoot as Billie Peetom nailed her second strike in a row. Dorene hadn't looked too thrilled when he'd announced he was going out, but he'd already told Cosmo he would sub for him as coach of the Hair Pins women's bowling team while Cosmo paid a visit to his in-laws in Greece. Buddy'd left Dorene, a.k.a. Cat Woman, lounging on his bed, chewing splinters out of a toothpick, with nothing ahead of her but a long, dull night. He'd set her up with a batch of pecan clusters cooling on the rack, but apart from that, what could he do?

The Hair Pins were a group of women aged twenty-four to fifty-three who, though they worked at competing hair salons, came together every Tuesday night to bowl as one stylishly coiffed team. They even had their own mini-bus, which transported them to tournaments in other cities. As coach, Buddy was required to drive the bus, picking up and later depositing the bowlers back along a ten-mile route. There wasn't a thing to coaching, Buddy learned, since these were professionals, if not in aptitude then at least in their attitude towards the game. There were some with arms lean and taut with muscle who could really put wings on a ball, and it was worthwhile to see. Cosmo had filled them high with strategy and the scoring was computerized, so, as Buddy saw it, his job was to cheerlead and to stop any fights from breaking out between his and the other teams. The Hair Pins were known for flinging lip.

Buddy sat down on the bench in front of the lanes with a cup of hot coffee from the snack bar, beneath the whirring fans of the Bowlerama, beneath the bug zappers with their cool blue glow and the sparks and crackles that meant they were doing their job killing insects, and he gave the thumbs-up sign as he saw fit. He found himself intrigued by the different body shapes the women had, and his spare thoughts, the few left over from the problem of his houseguest—whom he strangely felt he was being unfaithful towards—were occupied pondering what all was underneath their team T-shirts and shorts. It was the stringy, athletic ones like Vinia Hoogstrat or Marion Larson, who bowled braless, or the twins Dixie and De Lois Estes, Buddy thought he could picture most accurately, since they were, he figured, the female casts of his own body type.

Dixie Estes, the twin with the gray streak at the front of her hair, loosened up on deck by performing a series of lunges, hurdle stretches, jumping jacks and tai chi moves. Dixie was prone to bowling splits, and some of the Hair Pins, Jude Bensen in particular, made it hard for her to keep her confidence level up where it ought to be if she had any hope of scoring above the team average. They picked on her. When confronted, they insisted it was tough love and that Buddy was present *temporarily*, he should recall. Butt out, he heard. If she missed the pickup on the split, Dixie would have a small fit of temper in which she would stamp her foot and then kind of spin around on it so that her back was to the pins. For some reason this got to Buddy, or maybe it was the little ankle socks she wore with pompoms at the heel. Either way, he had a newly tender soft spot for Dixie Estes, so when Jude Bensen yelled, "What game are you playing? Field goals don't count!" he hollered back, "That's all right, that's okay, we can beat 'em anyway!" For Dixie's personal benefit.

The tremor in her bottom lip as she plunked down beside him on the bench, her thigh touching his, was not lost on him. "I wish that woman would act her age and not her shoe size," Dixie grumbled as she took over Buddy's cup of coffee, sipping it through the crack he'd made in the lid, like he'd only been holding it for her the whole time she bowled. She watched her twin pick a marble-swirled ball from the chute, thrust her fingers into it and heft it to her chest while she concentrated down the lane. De Lois let go the ball smoothly and it went like greased lightning, slammed the headpin straight on, and she had her own nasty 7-10 split.

Right away Jude Bensen yelled, "Oh my God, it's genetic!" inciting peals of laughter from both teams.

"Now to me," Dixie said, loud enough for Buddy to hear her over the rumble of balls and clash of pins, "that looked pretty good form. De Lois and I are used to being our own team, period. We're considering other athletic options as we speak. We may jazzercise Tuesday nights, or fence. You see, De Lois lives on the frontline of her own life and to her everything is personal. Insults hit her like bombs. Being a twin, I have to duck."

"Laughter, depending on its root, is not always the happy release it sounds," Buddy said.

"That's so true." Dixie agreed, her voice choked by emotion.

Before they left the bowling alley, a bunch of the Hair Pins gathered around Buddy and held an impromptu conference on the state of his hair. What could be done about it? Each woman, it seemed, had a different take on the way it should be cut and/or styled. Jude Bensen was bold enough to pull a pair of manicure scissors from her purse and lop some strands off the back to illustrate what she had in mind. Vinia Hoogstrat took the scissors and chopped more off the front. The result was a big joke, apparently. Buddy swatted the women away. They soon switched from arguing about his hair in concrete personal terms to arguing about hair in the abstract; the value of certain gels and mousses was hotly debated.

Dixie gave Buddy a coupon entitling him to a free cut and blow-dry at the Uni Cutz salon where she worked, since he was now a prime makeover candidate. She told him if he came in while she was still in the mood for it, she'd throw in some face patterning at no charge. She saw him, she said, with a goatee and sideburns or, failing that, minimal stubble. She tried to get the scissors to fix up his hair in the meantime, but Buddy wouldn't let her.

"You just can't leave it like that, hon. You look like you were groomed by a weed whacker."

"It's fine," Buddy mumbled.

"No, it's not. We've got to get rid of that beard too. You look scary."

Buddy glared at her.

"Really scary."

Boarding the mini-bus outside, Dixie asked if Buddy cared to join her and De Lois for a drink after they dropped the other Hair Pins off.

"How much does it matter to you where we go?" De Lois quizzed Buddy.

"Not so much," Buddy said, fingering his cropped hair.

"Good. Finally a man who's willing to float like a dandelion puff where the wind takes him," De Lois said. "I've been dating married men who are not that flexible as a rule. Adventure scares them but they all want to be tied up. Who am I to complain? They've always lived for tomorrow, not for today. An affair is a shock to their system some of them can't handle. But you know they crave it, living on nerves and such sweet pain. Lying to the one they love, lying next to the one they don't. We better take your car. It wouldn't look right to park the Hair Pins' bus in front of where we're going. We have to protect the team's reputation." She winked at Buddy and lit a joint that got passed around the bus.

At the warehouse lot that one of the women's husbands had donated as a storage depot, they traded vehicles. The threesome wedged onto the seat of Buddy's pickup, Dixie pressing in the middle, up close and firm against him, skin to his skin.

"Hang a left at the lights," De Lois directed.

Buddy drove to a bar called French Kiss, with neon lips on the outer wall, that featured male go-go dancers on Tuesday nights.

"Easy Rider is my new boyfriend," De Lois said. "Wait till you see his calves. They're spectacular. The rest of him looks like Lyle Lovett, Julia Roberts's new husband. Shoot me if I'm bragging."

"De Lois, are you stunned? Buddy doesn't want to watch men strip." Dixie nestled even closer to Buddy to show her support. "Anyone else have the munchies?"

"He said he doesn't care where we go. Isn't that right, Coach?"

"Don't let her push you around, Buddy. We can go someplace else if you want." Dixie peered at him intently.

"No, we can't," De Lois said, pinching her sister's thigh. She snapped open a compact and dabbed powder on her shiny spots, dulling them.

The women continued to bicker in the French Kiss parking lot while they applied makeup and sprayed perfume that caused Buddy to lean his head out the window and gulp for air. Dixie pointed out that she was getting sick of tucking dollar bills into Easy Rider's elastic G-string to keep him dancing at their table. Why, she wanted to know, if he was De Lois's boyfriend, didn't he dance at their table for free like any normal boyfriend would?

De Lois came back with the fact that Easy Rider danced for business, not for pleasure. It was his job, after all. Besides, he probably thought it would set a bad example and might even get him in trouble with the management. Anyway, he needed to pay his law school tuition somehow. She didn't mind contributing to his college fund.

Dixie groaned. "But that doesn't add up. You can't afford Easy Rider. Something is very wrong with your relationship when he's a constant debit."

"He's not a debit. Take that back. The thing is, you're right. I know if it weren't for his calves, I'd be able to resist him. You should smell him, Dix. Musky, salty like a slap of ocean, the way men used to be before deodorant soaps changed everything."

"No thanks. You sure you don't mind, Buddy? De Lois can't help herself—she's been bitten by the love bug."

"Love?" De Lois said. "Who said anything about love?"

Buddy looked from one twin to the other. They were both sulky and moist. Double trouble, he warned himself. Dixie pushed her finger into a little pot of lip gloss and applied it to her mouth, making her lips glisten like they were soaking, wet or just licked. Danger, Buddy thought. Slippery when wet. He shrugged, and what the shrug meant was he didn't know. He didn't know if he minded or not. He didn't know why, when he was around women, he shrugged so much. He didn't know why he was going to watch men strip when there was already a stripper in his apartment. He didn't know why there were so many strippers in his life all of a sudden. He just didn't know.

"Okay, then," Dixie said.

"Wait, give me a comb, Dix." De Lois took the comb, slid it across her tongue and then tried to pull it through Buddy's hair. "What did those girls do to you, Coach? How'd you get so many snags? Hold still, don't be a baby now. You ought to let Dixie do something with this mop before you end up with no choice but a marine buzz cut. It's a lost cause right now."

"He knows. I told him already. Although I have a nicer way of putting things than you do. I believe in hinting."

"If you want to live in the fast lane like James Dean, there's no time to hint. You'd be hinting and miss a sharp bend in the road. Dead, before you could spit out what was on your mind."

"Nobody wants to wed a morbid person, De Lois. You better improve your attitude, whitewash your personality."

"Smiling causes wrinkles. I am not in the hospitality business."

"You could have fooled me."

The bar was dark and two-tiered, with a runway surrounded by tables. Women of all ages and sizes were packed around each little table, laughing and drinking, smoke hanging in clouds above their heads. It gave Buddy goose bumps to hear them whistle and feel their eyes on him. De Lois picked out a table with a view and ordered a jug of house wine. When the music pumped up and the emcee came on, De Lois banged on the table with her hand. "Hey, boys," she yelled at the half-naked men prancing up and down the runway, wearing tiny sequined bags, flopping up and down to the music. Easy Rider wore a leather choker and motorcycle gloves as part of his wardrobe.

"That's him," De Lois yelled when she saw him. "Keith!" she hollered, waving her arms as though she was drowning or had broken down at the side of the road. "Over here, baby!"

At intervals the men would dance off the runway and onto the tops of small platform boxes, getting up close and personal to the women who clapped and stuck dollars into G-strings. The music throbbed and the men humped the air.

"He's coming!" De Lois screamed.

Easy Rider leapt onto a box near them, nudging their table and causing wine to spill over the rims of their plastic wineglasses. De Lois seemed bent on having a conversation with her boyfriend while he danced, but Easy Rider kept cupping his ear and shaking his head to mime he was deaf to her. Finally, De Lois leaned back in her chair so she could see his face better and sipped her wine. Buddy kept his eyes fixed, mostly, on Easy Rider's feet and ankles, which were covered with thick dark hair. The hair went up the tanned legs as far as Buddy was willing to follow it, and he noted that the calves were, actually, muscular and well shaped. Whenever Easy Rider thrust his bulging bag her way, De Lois shoved money into it, letting her fingers poke around in there. By the time Buddy left, the G-string was overflowing and De Lois was droopy-lidded with lust, her teeth biting into her bottom lip.

Outside, Buddy felt drunk, though he wasn't. Normally, he would go home, climb into his adjustable bed without brushing his teeth, clap twice to turn off the lights and be asleep like a lamb. But Dorene was there. He resented that he might have to talk with her, recount where he'd been and who he'd been with. He didn't care to debate with her how the pliant future might be skewed by the night's events. He didn't care to wonder the entire night through whether she was sleeping or lying awake. Comfortable or tossing fitfully. Were her dreams kind or were they tormenting her, softly, gently while she slept?

Buddy drove, detouring to pass by BoBo the caged black bear—something he'd taken to doing lately. The bear was there rain or shine; it was going no place. Buddy pulled onto the shoulder of the highway, dimmed his headlights and shifted the pickup into neutral, but kept it running. A hard flood of light shone down from the LIVE BEAR sign and he could see the dark mass of the bear hulked at the back of its cage. On the grassy area out front, two teenagers stood just beyond the illumination. They were waving bottles of beer, their arms wrapped around one another, their hot tongues fooling with love.

Buddy had the window rolled down and ribbons of swampy night air breezed against his skin as he drove on. When he saw a phone booth, he stopped and dialed Cheryl's number. Though he'd lived with her all that time, it came to him that he'd never really gotten to the heart of her. She was not an intimate person, but someone who always held back some essential part of herself. He didn't know her and she didn't know him, either. He considered this now with a fresh, stinging sadness that surprised him. They had met for drinks once after they'd separated and ended up in her new brass bed together. They'd made love, exploring each other almost as if there was a chance they might fall in love. When it was over, Buddy had regretted it as a step backwards, a wrongward leap away from the image he had of himself standing alone and untethered. Honestly, he never dreamed of hearing wedding bells ring, never cared about climbing any ladders. At the door, he'd heard himself telling her how sorry he was, that it shouldn't, and would never, happen again. "You bet it won't," Cheryl had said, and Buddy had glimpsed real tears in her eyes for an instant.

"Cheryl?" Buddy said into the phone. "What's the matter with your voice?"

"I just cracked my teeth. I was eating ice cream and drinking diet hot chocolate back to back, like I always do at this time of the month, and I have gone and cracked my teeth. It's a disgusting sensation I hope you never experience. I may be toothless before Toomer comes home—if he comes home. We had an awful fight over a spider. Toomer wanted to kill it, I wanted him to get it on a paper towel and throw it outside. He killed it and I guess he was right. I was trying to punish him after by making him clean up Lula's vomited hairball while it was still warm. For a big man with only a few working fingers, Toomer can't abide conflict. It gives him a stomach ache. Plus, he doesn't like cats. So off he went clutching his gut, banging the screen door behind him.

"You know that he has a little girl. She was born out of wedlock, and when he's upset, he drives by the house where she lives and looks up at her window and pictures her in there coloring with crayons or dressing a doll or something. He says it's as amazing to him as baseball-sized hail that he knows the word *daughter*, the most beautiful word in the dictionary, and what it means. Her name's Roseanne May Margaret. Toomer doesn't see her that much in person but he drives by her house a whole lot.

" 'Toomer, baby,' I've said to him on occasion, 'why don't you just go up and knock on the door? Maybe you could sit on the porch beside little Roseanne and talk to her a while, touch her hand if you wanted to.' You know what he said? He said, 'Sis'—he calls me that—'Sis, what if I'm sitting out there on the porch next to her and that hard old doll friend of hers, smiling my best smile when she says, so I have to bend over to hear, "Mister, you're a true big stranger to me and Tiny Tears. We think somewhere along the road you took a wrong exit; you followed all the wrong signs. From this distance, you're but a dusty cutoff in our eyes."' Poor Toomer's probably staring up at her window right now, hardly breathing for love and longing."

Cheryl sighed. "I make myself so sad sometimes. It can't be healthy. Some days I swear I feel my heart clawing at my soft interiors until I'm a wreck. How'd it go with your stripper, by the way? Any poop on her implants?"

"Stripper?" Buddy said. He bounced his shoulders up and down nervously, trying to ease the twinges dickering with his spine as he launched into a lie. "She did her business, a snappy routine, and left. I don't know to where. Could be anywhere—prison—you name it. The world is sprawling and far-fetched. If you wanted to, you could spend your time running in circles around it."

"Hmm," Cheryl said. "If she didn't bring up her implants, they must be anchored tight for now. Sick people are hopeless about spewing gruesome details and medical jargon. They forget to be embarrassed the way they're supposed to be about their bodily functions and could give a hoot for the rest of us still trying our best to be discreet. Toomer, for example, would love nothing better than to make me listen to what it's like having a thick spike in your finger and leeches grazing the length of your arm. But the thing about sympathy: it gets harder and harder to dish out. It gets to be old news. Speaking of which, I've got a pile of newspapers here stacked to the ceiling. I was thinking about making a papier-mâché fruit bowl and wondered what you thought. Is it do-able? My mother still uses that sweet candy dish you made for her sixtieth. It's right where you saw it last, still sitting on top of her television set, full of M&M's covered in dust because nobody will eat them because they're covered in dust. I bet you've advanced way beyond bowls now."

Buddy waited a second or two before answering, because sometimes with Cheryl what seemed like it was your turn wasn't.

"Buddy?"

"I'm making a pigasus," he said. "Last week in my craft class we picked our final projects, blindfolded, out of a hat and I got the pigasus. This extra fat pig with beady eyes and tiny wings meant to exaggerate its lumpen size, the impossibility of flight. You glue bright feathers to the wings before you hang it from a tree branch or specialty stand as a yard decoration. There was a pig collector who got so disappointed when I chose the pigasus that she called her daughter to come and take her home at the coffee break. I wish I'd known. I would've swapped for her mermaid, gladly."

"I think papier-mâché exists in that gray area between art and recycling—a nineties topic I'm hot on. Peter Jennings says we all make tons of garbage and we should be ashamed of ourselves and jump on the recycling bandwagon. At one point, I thought he was going to spit or cry—you know that look he gets. I dropped him a note to tell him not to slouch and to worry about his blood pressure. 'Imagine the havoc all this bad news must be wreaking,' I wrote him in neat block letters so he could read it easily. 'Smile more, Pete, and keep your chin up, literally. If I were you I'd try reading only good news once in a while. Take a viewers' call-in vote, but I bet everyone will agree it would make a nice change.' The only paper I had lying around was a get-well card, so the picture of the teddy bear with his arm in a cast wasn't great. Still, if you look closely, you can see where I rubbed out Toomer's name and a sexy message to write Pete's new one in pencil. If he wants to, he can use the card again, which is the beauty of lead.

"Thank God! Toomer's home!" Cheryl dropped the phone as she was hanging it up.

Buddy climbed back into his pickup. Home, he thought with

some puzzlement, a tricky concept. Not as easy a place to get to as you'd think. Like truth, or love, or fish, it was the only good thing in a pool of murk. Home had more to do with a man's own knowable center than any walls, pipes or trim in a building, he felt sure. He knew that home took real searching out, and after you'd found it, you had to remember how to get there no matter where you were coming from. The model home of Buddy's dreams was a bachelor unit, and he headed there instinctively, not unlike those stubborn pets he'd read about who walk a thousand miles through hail and sleet to get back to where they used to live.

ELEVEN

DORENE bolted up in bed, her heart banging against her chest. "Whelper?" she called after she found a voice, although it was not her own.

More pounding on the door. "POLICE! Open the door!"

Dorene leapt out of bed, only to freeze where she stood. There was no place to go; this was supposed to be her hide-out. She waited, caught like Bambi in the clearing, shivering so the hair rose on the back of her neck. Though even her own soft footfalls frightened her, she made her way into the closet. There, Dorene sat on her feet with her back to the wall, hugging herself. She needed to pee badly. Ten minutes went by, maybe longer, and nothing happened.

She began to wonder if this was some drama of her own imagination, brought on by a guilty conscience and the barbecue Pringles she'd eaten before going to bed. She chewed her lip. She would not allow herself to become one of those criminals who drove themselves crazy with paranoia until they confessed to everything, threw away their own key. Dorene knew her own worst enemy when she was stuck in a closet with her. She'd better hurry up and get used to feeling lousy about certain things but sunnier on the whole about others. She poked her head into the room. It was like being underwater, the silence pressing around her was so thick. She couldn't be sure if she heard voices or not. She guessed she'd stay put where she was a while longer. Ha. Where she was. Just look—her new life! Freedom!

Dorene felt herself teetering on the edge of some vast sadness so infinite that if she ever slipped and fell into it, she knew she'd never, ever get out. This is the point, she thought, when people give up, resign themselves to losing. Either that or it was the point when they got careless, tempted fate and risked everything because nothing was left to ruin or regret, past coming to their senses about anything because nothing made sense. They were *desperate.*

Dorene thought of her father. He'd been at that point when she was just a baby. Ready for the good, the bad or the ugly just so long as it was other than what he had. Didn't matter how reckless he had to be, dangerous, to get it. She figured that to him, her mother's love, and maybe her own such as it was at two months old, must have been manacles chaining him to a life he couldn't stand even to hate.

At the Mattatee County fair, they'd probably seemed a happy young family, there at the fair grounds with hundreds of others mostly to see the air show. But Destinee had been so occupied trying to nurse Dorene, who was colicky, she'd paid hardly any attention to the little yellow biplane with *Spring Fling '67* written across its side as it buzzed overhead, performing loops and dips, rolling, diving with its propeller pointed directly at the ground, then soaring up to become lost among the clouds. Dorene's father had been ready and waiting on the landing strip even before the plane touched down. He was the first to take the stunt pilot's offer of a ride to anyone in the crowd who dared to see the world from a new perspective, a bird's-unblinking-eye view. Destinee had watched from the bleachers as he paid twenty dollars and climbed into the passenger's cockpit for a fifteen-minute joyride.

The pilot had jumped behind the controls, pulled a pair of black goggles down over his face and signaled to two men to start the propeller. The little plane had lurched forward and lifted up, gaining height to circle the field once in a low swoop. The pilot had just begun his repertoire of stunts when the droning engine sputtered, then cut out completely. Destinee squinted into the sky; Dorene sucked irritably at her nipple. The little airplane had paused and hung motionless in the air for what seemed an impossible amount of time before crashing into a nearby potato field. Shards and chunks of yellow metal fell and were planted deep in the rich soil, shone from there like sunflowers. A picture of the field was in all the newspapers because it looked so strange and pretty—a flowerbed from another planet.

Destinee hadn't had any premonition of the crash that she'd understood. But when she ran, her baby wailing in her arms and herself also, to the site where a crowd had gathered, a retarded boy was yelling and making peculiar sounds. Exactly the same sounds she'd heard the night before in her dreams and not thought a thing about them. The newspapers printed a side story describing Destinee's psychic abilities, and from that day, the phone calls and the money poured in.

Dorene took one of Buddy's sweaters down from the hanger and gnawed a small hole in the wool sleeve. She worked loose a thread of yarn and pulled on it until the sweater began to unravel. She wrapped the yarn around and around her finger until most of the sleeve was gone and then she started on the body, wrapping the yarn tighter and tighter around her finger. It was oddly therapeutic, and remarkably, she found her mood lifting. She would look forward was all, keep the past behind her. True, it would be a hike getting from Buddy Whelper's closet to a stage in a nightclub somewhere, but she'd fix one eye on herself singing backup in a slinky costume and the other on the road ahead, and she'd get there. She wasn't the only person who'd set their sights on a distant, cloud-covered star and followed it, trusted it to lead them where they wanted to go. Ever since she was a kid, she'd wanted to be a performer. Not a stripper. Although maybe that urge to bare herself had been there all along. When she was six, Dorene had played Sleeping Beauty onstage and been so embarrassed by the applause that she'd lifted up her dress to cover her face. The audience had gone wild. Dorene had learned how to put a bold twist on her insecurities and it had become a kind of trademark. She opened the closet door a crack and threw out what was left of the sweater.

She was starting to breathe easier. Where were the police if they were so tough? If it was your only obstacle, how hard could it be to kick down somebody's door?

She pulled one of Buddy's plaid shirts off the hanger and put it on. It smelled faintly of sweat and a spice she couldn't identify, but the odor was agreeable, homey and male. Dorene thought of Buddy in the shower. He was something—a whole new species—standing there, soaping her from head to toe like he was a little nurse, and later, lying naked beside her on the bed, not doing anything to her, just listening. She could see him now. Picturing him so clearly, she was amazed to find herself becoming aroused. Sweet Jesus, as if she didn't have enough problems already without falling for a grubby hermit. Even though he honestly was *nice*, the only man she'd ever met who didn't have an ounce of conceit. She couldn't imagine how he'd be as a lover but she had an idea that he'd be better than she ever would have guessed. Better than Chad.

Buddy opened the door to the closet. He peered at Dorene crouched in the shadows, then at his sweater missing a sleeve and some chest. Dorene came out and stretched like a cat.

"It's you," she said.

Her hair was tousled and her lips were very red, as though she'd been biting them. Buddy saw that she had his clothes on, his shirt unbuttoned, and beneath it an undershirt through which he saw the buds of her nipples, deep, dark pink. Without warning,

Dorene grabbed him, pinning his arms to his sides, and squeezed him in a fierce bear hug. The way she had him, there was nothing he could do but wait it out. He could feel her trembling where she'd fixed herself to him but, when she let go, the tremble stayed and he had to wonder if it hadn't been his to start with.

"I'm going to wet my pants," she said, darting past him to the bathroom. In a minute, she returned. "I just made it. The police came while you were gone, that's why I was hiding. I was scared out of my wits. My nerves are loose wires. Hey, Whelper, you didn't send them to get me, did you?" The thought had just occurred to her. She tried to read something in his eyes. Guilt. But all she saw was clear-sky blue, sapphire blue, bluer eyes than any she'd ever seen in her life. God, they were beautiful. But his hair.

Buddy shoved his fingers through it and he could tell his hair had frizzed from the humidity. His ex would have subjected him to a hot—and she meant *hot*—Crisco oil treatment to tame it down. He tried to tuck it behind his ears, but it was cut lopsided, he guessed, since only one side went.

"You get in a fight with a pair of scissors, or what?" Dorene said.

"Sort of. The police weren't after you," Buddy said to deflect her from his hair. The pulse in his neck was jumping; his nerves were jangled too. "The lady in 2B committed suicide and willed her Amazon parrot to me. She left the police a note telling them to deliver it to my door. I guess because I paid it a compliment once. I told her, if it had been a person, it would have gone to college, because you could tell it was smart and eager to learn—which maybe no one had ever told her before—and so she took it as something important, regardless of how it was nothing but lip flap on my part. Proves you have to be careful what you say. You can't just throw words out, because they always come to land somewhere. And you don't know. They can land on a bleeding heart or a raw childhood wound, still open and in need of attention. The police left the parrot and a scribbly note right outside the door for anybody to trip over or steal, but it sounds like they knocked first, at least."

"Suicide is so sad," Dorene said. "This famous poet, I forget her name but you'd know it if you heard it, killed herself after her husband cheated on her. She had two little babies she left behind, sleeping in their beds. She put out two cups of milk and a plate of bread for them to find if they woke up hungry, then she sealed their bedroom door against the fumes and stuck her head in a gas oven. It always irked me what she thought they'd be hungry for. Bread or their mama, even if she was crazy? I guess leaving them that food was all she could do. They must have thought about it a lot as they grew up—what she meant leaving them a snack and taking herself away." Dorene picked up Buddy's unraveled sweater and hung it as best she could back in his closet. "You may have to wear something under this, Whelper, or join a punk band. Ha. You've got the hair for it."

Buddy was just coming to terms with Dorene still being there live in the flesh, since driving home he'd all but convinced himself she'd be gone, flown off to hide someplace else. He'd half hoped she would be. But it was the other half of his hope that rattled him. Lunatic hope.

"Let's check out the parrot," Dorene said.

Buddy followed her into the kitchen. The ornate brass cage was on the table, with the lime-green bird inside. Buddy didn't know why he knew, but he knew that a normal lifespan for an Amazon parrot was a hundred years. That perturbed him. He begrudged the bird an entire century on the earth—to do what? Spit pumpkin seeds and be of not much useful purpose. He wasn't thrilled either that the parrot might well witness his own last choke of air. Dorene put her face up to the bars and the parrot tipped its head, blinking. "Rhoda?" it wondered in a thin, strangled voice.

"No, baby," Dorene said, gently. "Your mama's gone to her reward. I'm Dorene and this here's your brand-new daddy, Whelper. He's going to take good care of you. Believe it or not, we were just saying how a little housepet might be just the thing lacking. What's your name, honey? Can you tell us your name?"

"Leonard, according to this note," Buddy answered. "*Leonard likes to sort shapes and look at himself in the mirror. He has a terrible temper. I think he misses flitting about the jungle. If you wrap him in a baby blanket and rock him faster than his own heartbeat, it'll calm him to sweetness again.*"

"Hey, Leonard," Dorene said to the bird. "You're so green."

"No kidding," the parrot quipped.

Dorene laughed, and it sounded so merry, Buddy laughed too.

"What else can you say, Leonard?" Dorene asked. "Do you have a nasty temper? You miss your natural habitat, high on the branch of a jungle tree?"

"Rho-daaa!" the parrot screeched, suddenly ducking to nip at something under its wing. "Good night, moon," it said, then stayed with its head tucked into its chest.

"He's cute, Whelper. Moody. I think he's tired after all he's been through. He's not making a whole lot of sense. He's snoozing like that, the silly. I wonder what happened to Rhoda—why she killed herself. Can I see the note?

"*Leonard is a big eater so don't scrimp his portions of parrot mix. If he asks, tell him 'Rhoda threw in the towel', then change the subject. He was the only happiness I knew, and even though he was expensive and people thought I was nuts, no one can tell me I didn't get my money's worth. Still, loving a parrot isn't enough. I am sad and have been since I got fat which led to other problems and now I'm fatter than ever. Big as a house, as my mother likes to put it whenever she gets the chance, which is often. I hope you'll rub Leonard's head sometimes for affection. You thought he was smart and you were right. Bye for now.*

"The 'for now' is scratched out, so I guess it ends 'Bye.' I bet Rhoda tried every diet in the world, which only makes you fatter, she probably didn't know. Poor thing. Your body starts storing each morsel you feed it when you diet, because it thinks you're trying to starve it to death. Bodies have their own armies which counterattack. It makes me nervous."

Buddy yawned. "I'll camp on the La-Z-Boy tonight," he offered.

"You don't have to," Dorene said. "I wouldn't want to steal your bed away from you."

"You wouldn't?"

"Well, bingo. That is the first snippy comment I've heard from you, mister."

"I'm tired, I guess."

"Go get your beauty rest, then, and thanks for the bed. Scoot."

After Buddy settled into the easy chair, he tried to settle his brain. What he wanted was a hard, deliberate sleep with no dreams, no options that might be presented to his subconscious while he wasn't available to resist them. In his mind, he pictured himself climbing into a small wooden boat. The air was soft and fragrant and he began paddling downriver into a perfect sunset. Then he heard a call, not of the wild, but of something too close for comfort. What he had been hoping for and dreading.

"Whelper, can you come in here a minute?" Dorene called, all sing-song.

She had lowered the bed flat as a normal mattress. Buddy hesitated, then sat on the edge where she patted beside her. "I won't bite you," she said cheerfully. "I was thinking, since we're adults and have seen each other naked, couldn't we just go ahead and sleep in the same bed? For comfort's sake. We don't have to announce it publicly. My feet are frozen."

Buddy got into bed beside her and they lay back to back until Dorene rolled over towards him. After a minute, she put her hand on his shoulder. She doodled her fingernail over his skin, which was pale and more velvet to the touch than it seemed like it would be.

"I know you'd rather I wasn't here, Whelper," she said quietly, "but all the same I'm glad for your kindness. I don't know where I'd be if it wasn't for you. You sure you don't have a girlfriend tucked away somewhere? She'd be lucky to have a man like you to share fun with, and bad times also. Don't you ever get lonely living by yourself?" Dorene stroked his hair. It was still mostly long as a woman's, but so coarse and thick it felt doubly masculine to her somehow. She knew Buddy didn't get lonely, not the same way she did. She could tell he didn't. Not the way she was even at this moment, tight in bed beside another person but as far away as she could be, alone alone alone. Dorene wanted all of a sudden for Buddy to look at her with his clear blue eyes and tell her the secret: how it was that you could be alone and not be lonesome.

"Whelper?" She tugged him onto his back. She pushed up on her elbows and leaned over him. He watched her, waiting. His cheeks and chin were dark with stubble, handsome in a rugged way she now thought, yes, he was handsome if you looked at him at this angle. His lips parted slightly, smiled. All her fond feelings for him rose to the surface, bringing a flush to her complexion.

In some remote station of her brain, Dorene was struggling to compute Buddy Whelper, sort through her sentiments. What was it about him, even though he was an oddball, that caused a strange affliction to begrapple her heart, an almost but not quite pain exactly that swelled rather than diminished when he was near? The truth, she suspected and secretly admitted, was that she welcomed the affliction, was happy for it, yearned for it to remain. She yearned for Buddy Whelper. God help her.

Buddy drew her down to kiss her mouth. Dorene felt his cock growing, warming up against her thigh until it was hard. Well, what did she expect, that they could just get in bed together and hold each other without it leading anywhere? There were hormones to consider, urges. Buddy cupped her face between his hands, and Dorene saw a tiny reflection of herself in his eyes. So maybe she wouldn't have picked him out of a crowd of men as her first choice. Still. A twist of fate had brought her to knock on his door, a stroke of luck she considered it now, and who could say that he wasn't what she needed if not precisely what she wanted? Buddy folded her in his arms comfortably and Dorene could feel herself give to him. It was as though, by his touch, he was setting right what had been spoiled in her. She was complicated, tangled as hopelessly as a person could get themselves in the course of a life, but maybe, if she let him, he'd help her straighten things out, simplify what needed simplifying, fix what needed fixing, until she was whole and of a piece again. She kissed his eyes, smooched the hollows of his cheeks, the ridge of his jaw, the skin behind his ear, like they were going out of style. She slid her hand down and eased him inside her. Buddy groaned. With every move of her hips, she felt more powerful. Restored.

Later, music swilled in Buddy's ears, Dorene singing to the all-night radio as he drifted towards sleep. Her voice was husky, pure and sentimental as feeling itself, blue and slow-tempoed, long-dawdling as a summer night. The notes filled him with care and want, picked him up and hurled him down again. Life was narrow, the songs told, it was dingy and sad but you had no choice; there was no graceful escape, so you had to make the best of it. Freedom depended on where you were coming from. There were cruelty, accidents and bad splits to get over. But there were wonders. Sparkling, take-your-breath wonders you had to admire and cherish for their strength and fragility. The words spoke to Buddy's heart directly. He believed the message floating up between the lines, rising like a dove, gospel above the rest. *This is all there is and ever will be. Tomorrow is out of sight.*

TWELVE

"DESTINEE, Ma, it's me. Listen, I'm in a peck of trouble. I need some money. Fast. I need you to wire me a heap of money. Ma? Oh, for pete's sake!"

Dorene stamped her Godzilla slipper in frustration and took a bite at her already chewed-up fingernail. What she wanted was to get some money so that when the time came she'd have independent means to prevent her from ever working for a pimp like Chad Delmonte again. She'd tried to make a living on her own before, support herself through her singing, but she wasn't that proud now or stupid. Money was just paper, and Destinee had been offering to give her some of it for years. Well, she'd take it, thank you very much, she'd stuff her pillows with it and see what happened to her dreams then. "Destinee?"

At last glance, Dorene had seen Buddy go into the bathroom toting a cookbook she guessed he was going to flip through on the toilet, and she was hoping he'd be like Chad and stay in there for ages. She truly felt bad about cramping his privacy. She found herself softly singing the Chris Isaak remake of "Solitary Man," her own musical interlude.

"Dorene?" her mother finally interrupted. "Sorry. It was that suicide case of yours, Rhoda, tying up my lines again. She's so happy and weightless on the other side, she's busting to talk my ear off. She says, by the way, to pass on that you should keep the curtains closed. Is everything all right, Dorene? You said you wanted money. How much do you need?"

"Heaps. Enough to start a new life without tacky costumes. I don't feel like prancing around as Little Bo-peep or Joan Wayne anymore. It zaps my spirit. Plus, I'll have to find a place to live and a job. I never heard anything back from all those demo tapes I sent out. I can't go into details now, Ma, but send a pile of money to the same place as before, when I didn't want Chad to know. Thanks. I'll write you a postcard for your fridge when I get somewhere."

"Dorene, wait. I was thinking something yesterday after Jack left. Not for good—he's driving his rig over to Tallahassee and then he promised he'd be back. I actually think he will be. Remember that sandpile you used to play in when you were little, under the old willow tree? I was sitting at the kitchen table with a mug of spiked coffee, Jack had been gone awhile, and I was thinking how, after the initial shock wears off, I actually don't mind being on my own. The quiet. Then I remembered you banging out the screen door. I heard it so clearly, the spring on that old screen door grinding and strumming open then slapping shut again. You must have spent a thousand hours building sand castles for the fairies to dance on in the moonlight. I'd slip out of the house after you were asleep and tinkle my fingers over the sand so that in the morning you'd see the prints and believe the fairies had come in the night and danced."

"I never said we didn't do nice things, Mama. I hope you're not going to bring all this up now. I had a happy childhood, Destinee. Kids are pretty tough. All I meant before, and I didn't think you'd dwell on it, was that you were so occupied, it was hard for me to get your attention. I always got a busy signal. It doesn't matter now. Your ears have their own requirements. Don't launch into a funk, Mama, please don't you. I forgot about those fairies. I sure envied them dancing every night under the stars and carrying on."

"Dorene, you know, sound waves never die. Every word we say, every sigh goes on forever, goes on, into the sky. Somewhere at the edge of the universe is a pocket where all the world's voices are kept in harmony."

Right after Dorene hung up, the phone rang, and she picked it up on reflex, then covered her mouth.

"Buddy?" a woman asked.

Dorene was too curious to hang up. "He's still in the bathroom."

"Who's this?"

"Who wants to know?"

"Dixie. I'm his hairdresser."

"Jesus, I didn't think he had one. Was that you who butchered his hair the other night?"

"That would insult me except the answer is no. I haven't cut his hair professionally yet. That's one of the reasons I'm calling. The other is to remind him about the Hair Pins' rummage sale. Donations have to be designer labels, no junk, since it's a 'designer' rummage sale. It's probably unlikely Buddy'll donate anything, but he might want to come. We're fundraising to buy the team matching bowling bags. You could give him the message."

"I don't know. He might not listen to me, I'm just his sister," Dorene said.

"Well, is he out of the bathroom, I'll tell him myself?"

"I'll check," Dorene said and hung up.

THIRTEEN

"GOOD MORRRRRNING," Leonard said in its tiny, shrill voice as Buddy came into the kitchen. The parrot was sitting on the roof of its cage, eating a grape. Dorene was scrambling eggs at the stove. Her ghetto blaster was playing new country music. On the table were two champagne glasses full of orange juice. Buddy blinked.

Cheryl had once taken him to see a show once called "Mystic Moments." In it a hypnotist took volunteers from the audience and put them into a trance by holding their wrists and then pulling on their arms, repeating "Deep sleep!" until they slumped over in their chairs like the air had been let out of them, sometimes leaning onto the stranger beside them. The hypnotist then suggested to the volunteer zombies that they perform various stunts and become various things—say, a human handcuff. When the hypnotist shouted, "Arrest that person!" the human handcuff would grab someone he'd never met around the waist and not let go until he was told he could. A plump young woman was transformed into Madonna whenever she heard a certain phrase, and strutted across the stage doing embarrassingly sexy poses that accentuated her ordinary, unglamorous looks. A young man was told Led Zeppelin, his favorite band, was performing a concert just for him on the front of his T-shirt, and he got his lighter out and held it in the air above his head, flame burning as he sang dismally offkey to words no one else heard, the fingers of his other hand ripping chords on an air guitar. Everyone had a big laugh at their expense, except Buddy, who was humiliated on their behalf. He was profoundly disturbed by the way the people gave up their own natures, betrayed themselves to change into what they were not naturally or comfortably. He'd seen nothing to do but get sloshed on beer and whiskey until he'd made, as Cheryl was happy to inform him the next day, a bigger fool of himself than all the others put together, who, at least, had been hypnotized as an excuse. He thought of it now because there was some echo, some thread that related to his current state of mind, though the significance of it, the reason for it, was well beyond his grasp.

"Where did you manage to find champagne flutes?" he asked Dorene, his gaze slowly moving from the glasses to her. Dorene had to turn the music down to hear him repeat the question.

She shrugged. "Stood on a chair and snooped around. All the pretty things are at the back of your cupboards for some reason, except for a million weird little bowls."

"Papier-mâché," Buddy said. "I made them."

"No kidding," she said. Impressed, he thought at first. "How come?"

Buddy frowned. Dorene's foot was tapping the linoleum in time with the country music on the station he actually listened to himself. The singers were known by their first names, the old and the new stars alike—Loretta, Tammy, Wynonna, Dolly, Crystal, Garth, Clint, Randy, Dwight, Hank, Billy Ray, Reba—as though they were friends or close relatives you could get right down to it with. Maybe it was a phony kinship, but Buddy had to hand it to them, they made you feel you weren't the only one with a tear in your beer.

"I hope you don't mind that I let Leonard out of his cage," Dorene said. "He asked to get out himself, in that funny baby voice of his. He asked for a grape too. It's strange having a pet that can talk to you and tell you what it wants. I feel like Dr. Doolittle. Sit down, Whelper, your breakfast's almost ready."

Buddy sat and watched Leonard waddling around the top of its cage, playing games with its grapes, rolling them with its bill and peeling the skin off before eating them. The parrot had four toes—two went the proper way out in front of it, the other two pointed back behind. It looked alien and grotesque, and made Buddy think of the scene in *The Exorcist* where Linda Blair's head spins around until her face is over her back. Not that Buddy was the best one to judge toes. He wriggled his own in the habit he had of checking every so often to see if he had regained any power to move the ones on his crippled right foot. He hadn't.

That foot had been mashed to a pulp when a customer at the Chrysler dealership had gone to test-drive a car but by mistake had set the vehicle in reverse and had backed up over his foot before he could jump clear. Buddy had pounded on the trunk and hollered and cussed, which had prompted the woman to shift carefully into park and get out to see what all the commotion was about. When she saw him pinned with his foot under the tire, his fist bloody from slamming the metal into dents, she'd burst into tears and run off the lot. The true piece of bad luck, though, was that he'd gotten run over on the lunch hour of a sunny Friday afternoon when all the other salesmen were gathered at a sports bar. By the time Buddy was rescued, he'd suffered a second-degree sunburn and his foot and ankle had broken in a mess of places, been crushed in others. What he had now was as good a replica of a human foot as the doctors had been able to scrap together from the bits of flesh and bone left for them to salvage.

Dorene pushed a plate of eggs in front of Buddy. "I put paprika on them to cater to your gourmet tastebuds." She didn't appear to be having any herself and took turns instead sipping orange juice and coffee. "Go ahead, before they congeal. I mostly only have liquids in the morning. Blame it on those Carnation Instant Breakfasts Destinee always made me as a kid. She'd mix it with water instead of milk because we were always out of milk. She'd drive to the supermarket and get so distracted by voices in her head that she'd forget what she'd gone there for—namely food. Coffee?"

"Uh-huh," Buddy said with his mouth full.

Dorene stood to pour him some coffee and she caught him looking at the convict costume she was wearing—the one she'd worn during their initial encounter when she'd stripped it off—and she glanced down herself. She gave a bitter snort of laughter. "The newest style from Paris," she mocked, sucking in her cheeks and posing like a fashion model. "I used to think this was cute. Ha. I'm getting heaps of money wired to me from Destinee and I can't even go out and buy a new pair of jeans or some underwear or a toothbrush. The list goes on. For once, I really haven't got a thing to wear." Dorene started to laugh but then stopped because it wasn't funny. "Maybe I'll take turns being Joan Wayne and Cat Woman the rest of my life. Little Bo-peep on Sundays and holidays. God, what a mess."

"I'll take care of it," Buddy said. "I'll get what you need."

"You will?" Dorene said. "How do you plan to do that?"

"I'll surprise you," Buddy said.

Dorene took a sip of coffee. She fixed her eyes on Buddy's face. "I just bet you will," she said. She held her eyes on him so long he would have been uncomfortable had the scrutiny not been as fond and warm as it was. "You know, Whelper, I've never met anyone like you. You're this scruffy cave man who comes at things the long way, but really you're very sweet. You're not selfish or mean—in bed, either. I don't know what to make of you exactly. You've got all this hair and these baggy clothes hiding you, but you shine out. Don't you just shine through like a glint of summer day."

Buddy was embarrassed but he knew that if he tried to deny

any of it, she'd only heap more compliments on him, becoming ever more flowery in her praise to try to convince him she meant her words. He shrugged.

"You're welcome," Dorene said and reached over and caught his face between her hands, kissed his lips, soft at first then with growing pressure. It seemed to Buddy she would have kept on, intended to keep on until who knows, if Leonard hadn't whistled at them, which broke her up.

"Leonard wants a little sugar too, don't you, baby?" she said to the parrot, blowing it a kiss. "Hey, I have an idea." Dorene tugged Buddy into the bathroom. "Close your eyes."

"No. I don't want to," Buddy said. "Please."

"Oh, for heaven's sake. Trust me, Whelper." She sat him down on the rim of the bathtub. "What do you think I'm going to do, slit your throat or something?" Dorene soaked a towel in hot water and wrung it out. She laid it over Buddy's face. "That feels nice, I bet." She straddled his lap delicately and sat on him. She removed the towel and lathered his face with menthol shaving cream, began to shave him with a sharp razor, pulling the skin tight along his jawbone, his upper lip, his neck. Buddy mugged his face in ways he thought might make the job easier for her. Every now and then she leaned to rinse the blade under the tap and Buddy felt the soft rub of her breast against his chin. It came as a shock when she said, "Ta da!" and lifted up off him, slapped some cool-stinging after-shave on his cheeks, a powerful musk that made his eyes water and that he didn't know he owned.

"Wow," Dorene said. "Look in the mirror."

"I can't. I have to go."

Dorene's eyes turned sappy and she said, "You look beautiful, Whelper. Let me do your hair now, too. I can't flub it any worse."

Buddy did have an urge to be groomed, to tidy himself. But he worried where the urge had come from and that it had sprung so suddenly. Why was it that when he looked down at his unlaced workboots, pink T-shirt that had started out red, shorts encrusted with paint, he felt newly ashamed? He could use an overhaul. Dorene smiled at him encouragingly. The problem, though, was he doubted that he cared to groom himself merely for the sake of becoming neat, and he feared that somewhere—below the surface—his self-respect was being clobbered, the image he had of himself glossed over. He stood up.

"I guess that's a no," Dorene said. "What am I going to do all day while you're at work? I've got a low-grade cabin fever burning, making me demented. I guess I shouldn't feel sorry for myself. I sure am grateful to be staying here. I appreciate it, honestly. I'm just lonely. I keep wondering how I got so cut off. How did my life narrow so that I have to rely on the charity of a total stranger to save me? I ruined all my own natural resources. It's scary to think that only a stranger's kindness, a remote act of mercy, can rescue you. But maybe that's not uncommon. Maybe the comfort of strangers is all there ever is. A big, anonymous hand reaching out to grab hold of you because you're not as alone as you think, because someone else is always near enough the edge to see you fall off."

"I know what you can do to keep busy," Buddy said. He didn't think he could take credit for reaching out to save Dorene. If anything, he'd only been the nearest outpost to cling to when she stumbled. He was just there. Not a willing, blood-and-muscle hand, but a jutting branch, hard-rooted all but pointless.

Buddy set up a work space and got together the materials Dorene would need, while she hovered at his elbow, curious as a preschooler. He'd already constructed the frame of the pigasus and applied the first layer of newspaper to it. When he took the model out from the cupboard and showed her the picture of what it was supposed to look like finished and painted, its tiny wings brightly feathered, Dorene stared skeptically, chewing her bottom lip.

"What the hell is it?" she said in a fit of giggles.

"A flying mythological pig. A pigasus. It wasn't up to me. I would have chosen something else, a mermaid. Forget it, not everyone likes crafts." Buddy started to pack things up but Dorene brought them out again to match his speed.

"I didn't mean to hurt your feelings. Don't get huffy. It's cute, really." She pushed up her sleeves. "Come on, show me what to do." After a little more convincing, Buddy demonstrated how to tear the newspaper into strips, dip them in paste and lay them on the form so they overlapped just so. "Ick," Dorene said when she first put her hands in the cold paste.

But a while later, after Buddy had put on his miner's helmet and safety goggles and had come to tell her good-bye, she'd seemed totally engrossed and had barely looked up at him, her pink tongue caught between her teeth.

Buddy had to fumigate the stairwells before he went shopping for Dorene. He was trying out a new double-duty pesticide that was supposed to kill roaches and smell like a pine forest. Or a spring meadow, or a rose bouquet—he forgot which he'd ended up buying. He went outside to get it and the air hit his shaved face. His skin felt newly sensitive, raw and exposed, the finest lick of wind made him shiver.

FOURTEEN

BUDDY CROSSED the hushed, green lawn of the Trinity Baptist Church, cut through the smatter of patio tables and chairs set up for the bake sale, and realized that most of the blue-haired women were watching him suspiciously as they ate their cake and sipped their lemonade through fancy colored straws. Dorene had shadowed behind him, needing to escape the apartment for a breath of air, even if it was only the sooty dust off the floor of the pickup, where she intended to stay crouched waiting for him.

Buddy hadn't thought to change out of his workclothes or shower, and he knew he reeked of pine forest pesticide. He felt deeply self-conscious and shoved his hands further into his pockets, his gimpy foot lagging as he speed-walked towards the Rummage Sale sign and the arrow pointing down to the church basement. At the bottom of the stairs, the Hair Pins had set up a raffle draw with a sample of the bowling bag they hoped to raise money to buy for each bowler propped next to the raffle prize of a tub of gourmet popcorn. The basement smelled musty, and Buddy followed a hallway into a large room lined with tables heaped with clothes, others piled with household appliances. Manning each of the tables was a Hair Pin. Buddy stopped in the center of the room and looked around, flustered. He'd intended to get Dorene some clothes she could wear until she was able to shop for herself, but he realized he had no idea in the world what size she might take or even what she would want to wear when not in costume. He thought to go back to the pickup to ask her.

"Hey, girls! Look what the cat dragged in!" Jude Bensen yelled at him.

Buddy felt his ears burn miserably and saw skinny Marion Larson square her shoulders and stomp the distance over to where he was. She had a HELLO name tag on but instead of her name she'd written, "Don't call me, I'll call you." Buddy stared at the tag, unable to decipher its intent or shift his eyes from it.

"You want some help, Buddy? You are lost in space somewhere. I'm being my own echo," Marion Larson complained. "Earth to Bud. Do—you—want—some—help?"

"Yes," Buddy said. "I need some women's clothes."

"Dresses, you mean. Stuff like that?"

Buddy nodded.

"What size?"

He contemplated her. "Bigger than you by some," he said.

"That's likely, since I'm a size small, which is less than average. You want medium, probably. I am *below* the average height and *below* the average weight for my age group. Sometimes it bothers me being *below* average. It's a personal hardship."

Marion picked out dresses, blouses, skirts, T-shirts, jeans to show Buddy, giving him her opinions and advice freely. The colors were what he went by: blue, orange, beige. Only Marion corrected him—ink, pumpkin, sand, she told him they were called in ladies' wear. Buddy chose terra cotta, jade, coal, heather. He didn't take into account whether the colors matched or would enliven Dorene's skin. Ink, pumpkin, sand is what he went for. He got so into the spirit of what he was doing that he added, on his own, a sundress with straps that crossed at the back, a pair of denim shorts and a turquoise-studded leather belt.

As Marion handed over the last bag of goods, she whispered, "Snuggle the baby for me."

Buddy stared at her blankly, backpedaling.

"Your wife just had a new baby, right? I was trying to figure why you'd be buying her a whole new wardrobe. Didn't she just have a baby? A tiny dewdrop boy with long fingers and silver hair, eyes the color of sea. Congratulations."

"I'm sorry, I'm not married," Buddy told her and watched her attitude deflate.

"You're not? Oh. Too bad. It was something pretty I imagined."

Buddy was weaving through the bake-sale tables with all his shopping bags, frowning because he'd been the prick that burst Marion Larson's bubble, when Dixie waved him over.

"Look at all those bags, Mr. Rockefeller. You ought to get a Born to Shop bumper sticker," she said. "De Lois says I don't leave any mystery to my nature to spur a man's interest, since you can read everything there is to know about me on the fender of my car—where I've visited, who I vote for, the works. My fantasy is that one day my ideal man will be driving behind me and flag me over. Try this," she said, stuffing a piece of banana bread in Buddy's mouth. "I forgot the sugar, but I don't think anyone'll notice. I wasn't sure your sister would remind you to come by today."

"My sister?"

"You were in the bathroom. I'm going over to the laundromat to wash these clothes I just bought so they don't stink up my closet. You should tag along. I'm allergic to mothballs. Bee stings, also. You can't guess what a drag it is to know you could be stung and die at the whim of an insect. Laundromats are one of those places that make you sit still and think, flipping through old magazines like you've gotten stalled in a time capsule. I come out of there all news-warped and grumpy. You better come with me so I don't get morose."

Buddy walked with Dixie the few blocks to the laundromat, passing close by the pickup where Buddy was startled to see Dorene peeking out the window, not crouched down the way he'd left her. Her eyes dittoed his surprise, and there was something else he thought he saw, confusion maybe, annoyance—jealousy. Dorene slid out of view. The laundromat was situated right next to the Uni Cutz. Buddy paused when he saw the row of plastic heads in the salon window, each wig modeling a different hairdo. Sets of long, glitzy false eyelashes had been glued to all the eyelids, metallic silver and gold. Dixie pushed into the laundromat, ignoring the Uni Cutz completely since it was her day off. Buddy followed.

They were just putting their rummaged clothes into the washing machines, Dixie observing with interest that Buddy shoved only women's clothes into the soap-filled water, when Dorene walked in.

"Hey," she said. She had a ballcap pulled low over her face.

"Hey," Dixie said.

The two women looked at Buddy. He had no idea what he should do. He kept loading the washer.

"I'm Whelp—Buddy's sister," Dorene introduced herself, scanning the place to make sure they really were the only ones in there.

"Dixie Estes. His hairdresser."

I'm the monkey in the middle, Buddy wanted to say. He didn't know why Dorene was being so bold coming out of hiding.

"Well, Dixie. It's nice to meet you," Dorene said. "I wonder when, if ever, you'll actually get around to cutting my brother's hair? Maybe hairdressing is just a clever smoke screen for some hanky-panky between you guys. You'll note I managed to give him a shave already."

"I saw. It's too bad because I was going to shape the beard into a goatee like Charlie Sheen has. It would have suited him better. There are things only a pro should tackle. Buddy, you ought to consider sideburns, at least, before you take this clean-cut image too far. Even Easy Rider has sideburns— Oops, I promised De Lois I wouldn't speak his name again. For your information, Buddy has a coupon he can use whenever he wants at the Uni Cutz. I don't believe in bulldozing a person."

"The Uni Cutz—that place next door? Perfect. Let's cash in that coupon, Dixie. My brother can't go around looking like a bedraggled tomcat from now to eternity."

Buddy tried to protest, but he relented when Dixie agreed to cut his hair in the relative privacy of the laundromat. She seemed eager to get at him with her clippers one way or another, despite her soft sell approach. She went and fetched scissors and a comb and other supplies she'd need to do his hair from the Uni Cutz. Buddy sat in the chair Dorene pushed in front of a clothes dryer.

He watched his reflection in the glass of the dryer door, clothes jumbling across his face as though, he imagined, he was looking into the tumbled workings of his own head. Dixie draped him in a plastic cover and pulled her fingers through his hair, uplifting it, massaging his scalp.

"He's got great hair," she said over his shoulder to Dorene. "It's so long there's all kinds of options for styles. You want me to try a couple of things out?"

"I don't want a style," Buddy said. "Except shorter."

The women came and stood in front of him, their hands on their hips, sizing him up as though he was a lump of clay they were about to mold. Dorene whispered something to Dixie and she nodded. Dixie unwrapped a stick of Juicy Fruit gum, jammed it in her mouth and set to work. At the sink at the back of the laundromat she filled a plant mister with water and sprayed Buddy's hair until it was wet. It took her a long while to comb out the snarls with an afro pick. Even pumping on a detangling lotion didn't help the matted ends that she had to snip off before she could start the real cut.

When she stopped to transfer their washloads into the dryer, Buddy saw that the floor around his chair was coated with big nests of his hair. He felt strangely shy and uncomfortable looking at his own hair on the ground, the mess he was responsible for, and he felt an odd, begrudging yet intimate, gratitude towards Dixie for renovating his appearance with professional calm. She finished cutting with the scissors and applied a dollop of what looked like shaving cream to his hair, jabbed her fingers up through it so that when he touched it with his own hand, it was stiff and spiky.

"I'm inspired," she said. She huddled with Dorene, whispering again, then announced, "I have a special treat for you. Men neglect their feet. I bet you've never had a pedicure." Dixie removed Buddy's boots and socks. She shook her head in amazement. "Oh, dear," she said. "Well, I was right. Your feet are crying for some TLC."

"I don't think I like this," Buddy said. Dorene shrugged innocently.

"Life is snappy," Dixie told him. "You are practically obliged to try everything at least one time. Take the bull by the horns, which is what I'm going to do with your feet. I see a bunion."

Dixie filled a tub with water and poured an entire box of Johnson's Foot Soap into it. "Look," she said, pointing to bold type on the box. 'Soaks Away Foot Misery. Has Relieved Millions of Feet Since 1870.' I bet a lot of those feet were in worse shape than yours. Some of them had to be. It's hard to imagine."

"It sure is hard to imagine," Dorene said.

While his feet were soaking, Dixie spread out some instruments and little spongy pads in various sizes and shapes. She began by cutting his toenails straight across and nudging down his cuticles, which she advised him never to trim with scissors. She clipped away rough edges wherever she found them and buffed his nails until they glowed. She used a Dr. Scholl's Corn

File to sand down his corns, the bunion also. She used a Swedish Foot File to scrape his calluses. When she was finished, she sprinkled his feet liberally with Athlete's Foot Powder, although, she admitted, she hadn't identified any fungus as yet. She pressed little sticky circular pads onto his corns to protect them and allow them to heal. There was even a product she had called Toe-Flex, which was designed to separate crooked toes. Dixie wedged the skin-toned barges between each of the toes on his mangled foot.

"There you go, darlin'. Head to toe gorgeous."

Buddy was utterly dismayed to see that she was picking his nail clippings off the floor. "Thank you," he said, pulling his socks carefully over the stuck-on cushions. His workboots now felt two sizes too small and he hobbled to collect the clean laundry Dorene was folding into bags.

"Take care you both," Dixie called to them as they went out the door.

"Bet we will," Dorene said.

Buddy caught his reflection in the pickup's rearview. He looked good, slicked and polished. He'd be pleased if it wasn't for the creeping notion that he'd cheated himself somehow. He had the feeling that, like his worn-in boots, what once fit him didn't give him enough room anymore. He had the disconcerting sense that his feet were not touching solid ground, that this new, spruced reflection of himself was treading thin air.

They got back to Buddy's apartment lugging Dorene's parcels and boneless chicken breasts for the fajitas he was going to make for supper. Dorene skipped into the bedroom to check out what all he'd bought for her at the rummage sale and to try everything on. "I'll give you a fashion show, Whelper," she called.

Buddy was going into the kitchen to unpack the groceries, when he saw Leonard lying dead on the window sill in the living room, eyes shut, wings awkwardly bent. But then he got closer and saw the blue chest feathers rising and falling. Buddy shook the bird gently, meaning to wake it up if it was sleeping or for some reason only faking dead as a trick. Higher on the window pane there was a smear of blood that streaked downwards. Buddy looked for, and found, a crust of dried blood on the parrot's head. He hadn't considered that it might actually be capable of flying still, since in his limited exposure to it, he'd never seen it do anything more than try out a flap. The bird had seemed naturally inclined to toddle penguin-like wherever it went, and Buddy had supposed either its wings had been clipped or it had been trained to quit flying as an infant while kept captive in a South American jungle hut. Buddy turned as Dorene pirouetted into the living room.

"There were all these different colors, I hardly knew what to put together," she said breathlessly. "There's so much stuff. I love this turquoise belt. Of course, some of the things I wouldn't be caught—" She broke off and stared at Buddy as though, he thought, he'd just touched down in a spacecraft. "Look at you," she said finally. "I guess I wasn't really paying attention. Aren't you a picture?" She gasped in horror. "Leonard!" she cried, rushing to the bird and cradling it up. "What happened?" Her eyes were tracing the blood smeared on the window even as she asked the question. She rocked the green bird faster than its own heartbeat. "Did you do mouth-to-mouth?" she drilled Buddy.

Dorene was prying apart the bird's bill when its eyes flicked open and it let out a shriek so piercing Dorene echoed it back. The bird flapped and shrieked again and Dorene set it down on the floor, where it waddled frantically in circles, lifting and dropping its wings in a panic.

"Leonard, baby, calm down, sugar. Hush. Hush now," Dorene soothed in a mother's lullaby croon. "Jesus, that's why Rhoda wanted me to keep the curtains closed. Poor baby. I should have listened to your—"

"Rhodaaaa, Rhodaaaa," the bird took up calling, screeching its terrible screech, dashing in circles, flipping in half somersaults and rolling.

"He's having a fit, Whelper. Slap him."

Buddy stared at Dorene, then at the bird, but it seemed to be slowing.

"Wait! Don't hit him," Dorene said. "I think he's coming out of it."

The bird climbed Dorene's leg like a tree trunk, then her arm, until it was sitting on her shoulder. "He's back to normal," Dorene whispered, genuinely relieved. "I'm going to put him in his cage with some water." She snuck a curious, sidelong look at Buddy as she passed him, as though he was a handsome stranger. Either that or a dog that might bite.

Dorene came back into the living room decked in another outfit, a peasant skirt and a ruffled blouse. Her manner had turned very still and concentrated. Her eyes searched Buddy, in no hurry. "I didn't thank you," she said. "You know, that you took the trouble to get all these clothes, to pick everything out. You even did my laundry."

"I'm sorry," Buddy mumbled, "that everything's used. Secondhand. There's an iron around here somewhere." The clothes seemed more wrinkled than he remembered.

Dorene gave a small laugh. "There sure are a lot of colors, huh? Blue, orange, beige."

"Ink, pumpkin, sand," Buddy whispered.

Dorene stopped mid-laugh and regarded him more closely. Looking him in the eye, she felt a tenderness for a human being she had not felt in a long time. She put her hand against Buddy's clean-shaven cheek and stroked it admiringly. "I had you pegged, T. Buddy Whelper, as some crazy Grizzly Adams-type loner who didn't need to operate by the same rules as everybody else. I thought you were generous and kind, but odd, way out on the fringe. But now. You could be an ad in *GQ* magazine, hunk-of-the-month, all scrubbed pink and pretty. I didn't expect this. I wish I had some mascara and hoop earrings." Dorene sighed. She knelt down and took off Buddy's socks. They both studied his naked feet.

"Nice pedicure," she said. "It looks painful."

"It is. My boots don't hardly fit anymore."

"Welcome to the world of beauty. No pain, no gain." Then Dorene kissed him hard and full on the mouth since words were not ample.

Buddy marveled again at the precision with which she tailored herself to him, the give-and-take of their hard parts and their soft parts. He could feel Dorene's heart beating through his T-shirt, and when he took up trembling the way he'd done before, he knew, without a doubt, the pump-root of the tremble was within him. It was as though a spring of pure emotion welled at his core. It alarmed him how divided he was between what he thought and what he felt. Buddy knew he ought to watch out what he was getting himself into, and yet, quite at the same time, he felt that it was all somehow only normal and fated, no cause for concern.

"Oh, honeydrop," Dorene cooed, blowing the words straight into his head by way of the delicate, swirl-windy tunnels of his ear as she undressed them both with hurricane speed.

FIFTEEN

"I'D KILL FOR A CIGARETTE," Dorene said as the landscape outside the pickup loped past. She pushed the mining helmet back on her head and loosened the strap on the safety goggles she'd borrowed from Buddy so she could go out incognito. This time, though, she'd be careful not to let cross-eyed jealousy put her at risk. "Take me somewhere," she'd said to Buddy after eating a third yummy but smallish, she thought, fajita. Getting outside his tiny apartment and hitting the highway, those white lines on the road zipping by, made her want to roll the window down and stick her head into the wind, yodel at the top of her lungs. The world was waiting up ahead. She'd planned to venture out after dark, but it was too much. She couldn't stand another minute of Buddy rowing on his rowing machine, rowing and huffing and puffing and rowing, getting nowhere. It depressed her. She needed to get out. She'd had a taste of escape and she wanted more. She told Buddy to put his foot down, and the pickup shifted gears automatically. The sky was plum-colored, rich and light. Everything looked new to her, intensified, as though someone had taken a black marker and outlined it all—the trees, the houses, the telephone poles—so that each stood out and could be uniquely admired.

Buddy pulled off the road into a Gulf station mini-mart, stopping the pickup next to a self-serve pump. A sign on the top of it said PLEASE PAY INSIDE BEFORE FUELING. Just before Buddy went into the store Dorene yelled for him to get her a Snickers and a Crystal Pepsi.

He hadn't said a word about the money he'd picked up that Destinee had wired. Ten thousand cash. Which Dorene knew Destinee wouldn't have blinked an eye at sending. Buddy had given it all to her, entirely it all, and she'd had to make him tell her how much he'd spent buying her clothes at the rummage sale so she could pay him back. The problem was, the things had been so cheap and the smallest bill she had was a hundred. Since Buddy couldn't or wouldn't make change, and he wouldn't accept more than he'd spent, Dorene just had to plan that when she got settled on her own somewhere she'd give him a tidy lump sum as a reward for his trouble. He sure was a stroke of good fortune. In her wildest dreams, Dorene couldn't have imagined a better person's life to crash into.

Buddy handed her the Snickers and Pepsi and wouldn't take money for them either, or the gas. She'd need her money, he told her, and ought not to let it burn a hole in her pocket trying to get spent.

"I'm keeping a tab," Dorene said, crumpling the candy wrapper. She twirled the dial on the radio and brought in a gospel station, Tennessee Ernie Ford singing "What a Friend We Have in Jesus." Dorene sang along. "I don't care for the message but I love the sound. I make Jesus a regular boyfriend when I sing gospel hymns. That's a secret. They can be corny and dumb but they let you show off a good voice if you own one. Destinee used to drive me to church sometimes, when I could coax her to do it, so I could sing in the congregation. I'd sing like an angel and I felt like one. Those songs washed over me, flooded me with happiness, the way the sun would beam in through the colored-glass windows. I might have liked to be in the choir, except Destinee would never have taken me that often. Now I think about it, somebody from the church would have given me a ride, but when you're a kid you don't realize options. You depend on your mother for everything and you wait, until you give up waiting and hook onto something you can do for yourself." Dorene sighed. She took off the mining helmet. "This thing's making my hair sweat." She took off the goggles. She smoothed her lap; the sundress had little purple violets sprinkled all over it. "Am I pretty?"

"What?" Buddy said and turned down the radio. He cupped his ear but Dorene didn't repeat what she'd said.

Buddy parked at the side of the highway, and at first Dorene couldn't tell what he was stopping for, but when he got out, she did too. He walked across the tall, sunburned grass, limping more than usual because of his pedicure and the rocky ground, towards a steel cage with a light fixed to its roof, shining down and out. She caught up to him and looked where he was looking. She had to squint to see the bear.

"It doesn't look 'LIVE,'" Dorene commented, picking up a stick and poking it into the cage and the bear's rounded back.

The bear was lying on its side, a paw covering its eyes as though the light bothered it. Dorene prodded it again and it flinched, causing a ripple to roll under its skin and a leg to shudder. She was about to poke it one more time to see what would happen, but Buddy said, "Don't. Let it alone, it wants to sleep." He took the stick from her and tossed it away up in the air. They both watched it cross the moon.

"P.U.," Dorene said, holding her nose and taking a step back from the cage. "Live bear, my foot. That thing smells revolting, it needs a body shampoo." Buddy hunched up his shoulders and made a point of ignoring her. Behind her, Dorene noticed a shabby snack bar, the lights on inside, two men with ballcaps sitting at the counter, talking to another man who was pouring them coffee. He had one set out for himself too. Dorene saw the steam rising from the three cups. Outside there were some picnic tables, hard to see in the growing dark.

"Hey, do you think it'd be safe if I went into that snack bar, Whelper, and got us some coffee?" Buddy was examining the rusted lock on the cage and only nodded briefly at her over his shoulder.

Dorene went back to the pickup and then tramped along the gravel shoulder of the highway to the snack bar. The men looked at each other when she walked in. She ordered two coffees to go, stared right back at them through the goggles, didn't care how they had to shield their eyes from the beam of her flashlight helmet. When she went to pay, she remembered the smallest bill she had was a hundred. She gave it to the man behind the counter anyway. He held it between his fingers and didn't move. The men all looked at each other again. Dorene rolled her eyes.

"What's in that bag there?" she said, pointing.

"Shrimp," one of the men said.

"I'll take that too," Dorene said. "Two coffees and that bag of shrimp. I hope they're fresh."

"Brand-new fresh," the man said. "Tasty with some fish sauce."

The man behind the counter put her hundred into his cash box and handed her change and eighty-nine dollars back, like each bill had glue on it that made it stick to his fingers and be hard for him to pass into her palm. Dorene stacked the coffees on top of each other and grabbed the bag of shrimp. But then the one man sitting down reached over and got the other man's pack of Camels. He shook out a cigarette and went to light it up.

"You don't want to do that, Earle," the owner of the Camels said.

"Do so," Earle said.

Dorene watched as Earle took a deep drag on the cigarette, his nostrils flaring as he sucked the smoke in, held it, blew it out in a long stream. His friend shook his head, sadly. "You won't never stop now. Once you start a dirty addiction like smoking you can't get away from it. Look at me. I dream about tobacco. I love nicotine like a big-boobed woman."

"Hey, Earle?" Dorene said. "I'm trying to quit and you're trying to start, why don't we let's split that Camel between us, so we won't neither smoke a whole one on our own?"

Earle's friend nudged him and said, "Ace idea, Earle. Give her a puff."

Dorene blew a chain of smoke rings.

"I can't do tricks yet," Earle said, jabbing his finger through the drifting circles. "I wish I could."

Dorene went over and put some quarters in the jukebox. She selected some hits and stood watching the 45s spin. She swayed on the spot to the music, singing and smoking.

"I love music, Earle. I love singing as much as I love smoking. I especially love when I can do them both together. Well, thanks for the snacks, fellas. Adios."

Outside, she sat on top of a picnic table and told Buddy to come get his coffee. He came and sat down.

"Thanks for taking me out, Whelper. You come here a lot, or what?" She pried off the lids from their cups, held her hand over the steam.

"Sometimes," Buddy said, absorbed in looking at the plastic bag on the table next to Dorene.

"You like bears? Zoos?" Dorene asked. "I guess they had other animals here once in those empty cages. I bet they all got flea-bitten to death."

Buddy picked up the bag, shook it a little and brought his face closer. When he saw shrimp, his eyebrows shot up and he put the bag back down on the table and blinked at Dorene.

"I nabbed us some seafood," she explained. "It'll be tasty with fish dip. So tell me, what's going on with you and this bear—what's his name?"

"BoBo. Nothing's going on. I don't know. The cage is too

small." Buddy took a sip of coffee and jerked the cup away from his mouth.

"Burnt your tongue?" Dorene said. "Poor baby. Why don't you tell the guy in the snack bar to make a bigger cage? Tell him you'll call the Humane Society if he doesn't. Tell him you'll picket."

Buddy shrugged.

"What?" Dorene said.

"I don't know." Buddy cleared his throat. "I don't know how big a cage I'd tell him to make."

Dorene thought. "Well, maybe he could get the bear to stand up with its arms in the air and then he could make the cage a smidge taller than that. Leave the bear some headroom to stretch. The same thing going sideways. That would be an improvement."

Buddy tipped his chair back and studied the night sky. Dorene watched him.

"I used to know about stars," she said. "Orion, the Big Dipper, the Dog Star. But I forget now which is which or what they're supposed to mean. I wonder if Rhoda's up there, peeking down at us from behind a silvery diamond, a dark cloud of heaven." And Chad, a voice inside her head asked, what about Chad? He might be watching too. Smiling to show off those glittering white teeth—starry teeth—a million miles away. "Stars are dead, you know," Dorene said. "They don't look it but they are."

"I don't know if Rhoda would have got up to heaven," Buddy said, "seeing she committed suicide."

"Hmm. Maybe not." Dorene drank her coffee, then her hand tightened around the paper cup, tightened and squeezed. Coffee erupted over and onto her sundress. "Oh, God! Whelper! I just had a brainstorm. Why didn't I think of this before?" Dorene tugged off the goggles and helmet. She bit her thumb between her teeth. "I'm free! I think. I think you're free, too. Wait." She tapped the side of her forehead. "What if Chad committed suicide? Like Rhoda. What if he went and killed himself instead of me having done it for him?" Dorene drank what was left of her coffee in thoughtful sips, working it through, while Buddy gaped at the sky.

"Okay, here's the plan," she said. "All we have to do—that sounds glib—but all we have to do is go to Chad's and plant a suicide note somewhere conspicuous. I'll forge it in shaky handwriting so it'll seem he was real upset when he wrote it. Good-bye, cruel world, blah blah blah. But there's a hitch. Two hitches, actually. First, Chad'll be naked. I think if you were going to kill yourself, even if you were going to be soaking wet in a bathtub, you'd wear clothes so you wouldn't be undignified in front of whoever found you and had to pull you out, zip you into a body bag. So we'll have to dress him. Probably you'd wear something you kept for special occasions, the blue suit he wore to his sister's wedding. Do you think that would be appropriate?"

Buddy gaped at her.

"Okay," she went on. "The second thing is, it's been a week. Just how bad do you think he'll smell exactly? See, what I'm getting at is, I wonder whether he'll even still be there or if we're too late and somebody couldn't help but notice him decomposing and broke in to fumigate. I guess we'll find out soon enough, won't we? I wish I'd thought of this from the start. But then I never would have met you. I sure am glad to have met you. Ready?"

"What—now?" Buddy said.

"Why not? I'll do the suicide note in the car. Lord knows, I'm in the mood for it after seeing that poor excuse for a wild animal."

But Dorene had a harder time than she'd expected writing her dead lover's good-bye message to the world. Twice she had to wipe tears from her eyes and stop herself from becoming poetic. It just went to show there was a trace of something good, nice even, in every bad, more or less, if you scrounged for it. It was a cruel pang to her heart to admit there were bits of him she loved, still. There was a wink of his she recalled fondly because it had come at an opportune time. She could see the wink. It was a keepsake prize she'd won off him for good. Another time, Chad had done a striptease, trying his best to be sexy, when he was first teaching Dorene how to do it. That had been some fun watching him prance around to music, swinging his dick like he might injure himself. But all and all, mostly, he'd been someone mean and bad to know. Turn, turn, turn, she told Buddy until they were idling outside Chad's apartment building, them both filling their lungs with clean night air before they plunged inside. Dorene led Buddy on, her breath hard-squeezed from her tight chest, struggling to keep her head above drowning as the elevator took them up on it.

SIXTEEN

INSIDE the pink-stuccoed apartment building with the clay tile roof, Buddy followed Dorene gingerly across Chad's plush, chocolate-colored wall-to-wall carpeting, so thick they left behind a trail of footprints in it like wet sand on a beach. The air-conditioning was humming. Two leather couches faced each other in the living room, one with a rumpled granny-squares afghan on it. Hung on the main wall was a series of coconut shell heads, loony, ghoulishly embellished. A whole village of coconuts—men, women and children—in all kinds of moods: angry, surprised, happy. A spray of plastic flowers in a bud vase decorated the coffee table between the couches. The sliding glass doors to the balcony were closed and covered in aluminum foil to reflect the heat away in the afternoons. Dorene's eyes were wide and glazed.

"Are you all right?" Buddy asked her.

"No," she said. Her face was pale except for two feverish patches that had blossomed on her cheeks. "I'm scared shitless. The scene of the crime and all."

Buddy towed behind her down a hallway to the bathroom. Dorene stopped before they got to it. "This one time," she said, "Chad and I were out driving in this clunker convertible he had. It was hot so I had my shoes off and my feet stuck out the side to catch a breeze. We got into a fight about a song on the radio. *On the wings of a snow white dove, He sends his pure, sweet love.* You know that one? Ferlin Husky. Chad said it was somebody else singing and I said no way, it's the man, Ferlin Husky. Chad told me to get out of the car. He practically pushed me out. The fight was about something else. The fact that I'd had the nerve to argue with him in the sanctity of his own car. He slowed down, reached over and slung open my door and shoved me out onto the road. He took off with my shoes. I never thought he might turn around and come back. I never thought. I watched that car get smaller and smaller until it was a dot, lost on the horizon. In the heat, the road tar was bubbling. By the time I hitched a ride, blisters had burned up on my soles and then rubbed off so there was no skin left on the bottom of my feet to walk on. Chad drove away with more than my shoes. What he took, I never really got back. But I walked on, didn't I? I'm walking on."

The door to the bathroom was ajar and the room empty. Dorene went inside and looked for a long time at the empty bathtub. She noted the drops of water in the bottom of the tub the same way Buddy did. She examined the damp towels on the floor, the tube of uncapped toothpaste on the vanity, bottles and jars of makeup, a can of shaving cream. The cabinet under the bathroom sink was stocked full of nothing but toilet paper, white two-ply. Dorene closed the cabinet door and shook her head from side to side. Wordlessly, Buddy followed her into the bedroom.

The bed was unmade, the sheets dingy. Dorene opened the clothes closet and ran her hand over a row of dresses hanging beside some men's shirts and pants. "These aren't mine," she said. She turned then and a framed photograph on the night table caught her eye.

"Ha," she said bitterly. "Look at this." She thrust the picture at Buddy. He looked at the photo of a tanned man in a three-piece suit, with gold chains showing in the open neck of his shirt. Beside him stood a shapely woman, almost naked, pale as a statue, except for a tiny triangle of cloth over her pubic area and tassels on her nipples. There was something familiar about the woman. Buddy looked more closely and, with a start, saw a fine scar across the neck where a different woman's head had been pasted to Dorene's body. The surgery was sloppy, part of Dorene's hair underlapped the other woman's hair around the edges, making the head seem too big for the shoulders, although that wasn't truthfully the first thing you'd notice.

"That's Chad and you, is it?" Buddy said.

"And Gloria." Dorene snatched the picture from him and flung it against the far bedroom wall.

"I always hated that picture. That's how Chad saw me, naked and tasseled, which is why he liked it. I knew when I first saw it, if I didn't know before, what he thought of me. I wasn't a backup singer to him, I was a stripper. You can't fool a camera. It sees what's there plain as day in front of it. Not like me." Dorene was crying now. "That chubby bitch, Gloria, glued her head to my body. Can you believe it? She's Chad's old flame. I don't get it."

Buddy put his arms around her but she shook him off. She stomped into the kitchen and stood glaring, ready to cause destruction. She banged open cupboards, dishes rattled. Buddy watched from the doorway as she removed a plate of pie from the fridge and let it drop so it broke, splatting cream, in the middle of the floor. She wrecked eggs.

"I was making pork chops once and Chad came up behind me. I still don't know why he hit me but the pork chops went flying out of my hands like sparrows. I remember crawling after them across the linoleum, thinking what a waste it all was. A pure waste." Then Dorene saw something that pulled her breath back through her mouth in a hard gasp. Trancelike, she crossed into the dining room. "God almighty," she said and sank to her knees.

A double stack of cardboard boxes had been mounted neatly, a dozen or so in total, Buddy guessed, almost to the ceiling. He read the packaging, which was the same on all the boxes. Each contained a Sony VCR. He turned to Dorene, who was rocking back and forth, both hands covering her face. Her head was wagging no. No, fast and not letting up.

"Dorene?" Buddy said. Then seeing her head wagging no, no, no, her eyes shot wide with fear, he grabbed hold of her. He kept his arms wrapped around her through her pushing him away, fighting at him like a child marooned in a tantrum, held on until she gave and folded against him. When she wept, he told her "baby, baby, baby" and other soft purrs to soothe her mind.

Finally, Dorene heaved a long, jagged sigh and mopped her tears. "Chad Delmonte is alive," she announced, pointing at the boxes of VCRs. "That's proof. He might as well be standing right there in the flesh. His other hobby, besides chasing women, is dealing stolen property. VCRs being his favorite commodity. Those boxes might as well have a mouth to grin mean, perfect teeth at me. God, what am I going to do? I killed him."

"Apparently you didn't," Buddy said, trying to yank her to her feet. If what she said was true, they'd better get out of there pronto.

"I saw the lights blinking. He wasn't moving. I killed him, Whelper. I heard the sizzle when I killed him. I was his murderer. I should have used a damn gun."

"There must have been a short circuit. Maybe a ground fault interrupter kicked in and cut the power. Chad got jolted unconscious but the fuse blew before he took enough electricity to kill him outright. Get up, girl."

"This is a nightmare. No matter what I do, I can't get free. I've been searching for my freedom but it's not anywhere. I can't find it anywhere. He killed my babies, Whelper. My dreams. Christ. What am I going to do?"

"We have to get out of here, Dorene," Buddy said. "Now." He was trying to think what it meant, the consequences if she hadn't murdered anybody and didn't have to hide out anymore with him, in his apartment. He dragged her to her feet.

"Okay," she said, taking a deep breath. "Here." Dorene handed Buddy a VCR box. "That son-of-a-bitch Don Juan asswipe. So Gloria's back in the picture, huh? I guess he got over her halitosis in a hurry. Guess he got to appreciate cellulite. Can you handle another one on top?" she asked, already picking up a box.

"What are you doing?" Buddy said as she plunked the second box in his arms.

"Taking some VCRs."

"Why?"

Dorene shot her eyes at him. "Because I want to." She loaded a third VCR on top of the pair he was already carrying and hoisted two more for herself.

When they got in the elevator, all the buttons were lit up. Somebody had pressed each floor number as a joke. The doors opened and closed all the way down, Dorene swearing every time. Out in the parking lot, she stumbled and dropped one of her boxes. While they were reloading them, adjusting the bulky items in their arms, Buddy heard a man shout, "Hey!" then "Hey!" again, louder and more vigorously. He looked up and spotted two men waving from a balcony just below the roof. "Hey!" they shouted, and other words he couldn't make out, lost on the wind. A dog barked dangerously.

Dorene was off running for the pickup. "Jesus H. Christ! Move your butt, Whelper!" she screamed.

Buddy ran for it, his bad foot urging him to go lightly with every pounding step, so that he hop-skipped along. They pitched the boxes into the back of the truck and jumped into the cab. "Lock your door," Dorene commanded, pushing her knob down at the same instant. "Floor it."

At first Buddy thought it would be fine once he hit the road, but it wasn't. A set of headlights veered through the traffic behind him, giving chase. Dorene saw him looking in the rearview, panicked and spun to look back herself. "Shit," she growled.

They sped up the ramp and onto the highway, the car following behind, gaining speed until it was right on Buddy's tail.

"Brake so they'll crash into us," Dorene ordered.

Buddy twisted his face and gawked at her like she was demented. The car swerved out from behind them with a screech of tires and got even, up alongside. Buddy peered down into it. Two shadowy men were inside, yelling, their faces contorted and cartoon-like, a dog sloshed on their backseat. Buddy's nervousness made him smile moronically at the bad guys. The man in the passenger seat motioned for Buddy to roll down his window and he started to, curiously removed from the action, everything slow motion.

"Are you nuts?" Dorene bellowed in his ear. "What do you think you're doing?" Her voice was hysterical, high-pitched. She leaned across him and gave the men the finger, bumping Buddy's steering arm so that the pickup swerved sharply. The other car copied the move expertly and there was no scrape of metal. Dorene squinted to see into its interior. "Roll your window down."

"But I thought—" Buddy said, rolling it down.

"Fuck you, Chad Delmonte!" Dorene screamed across him.

She grabbed a large wrench off the floor of the truck and hurled it out the window, barely missing Buddy's head. It was a good throw and hit the car's windshield dead on, shattering it. Brakes squealed and the car skidded, burning rubber to a stop, then crawled, a wounded beast, off to the soft shoulder. Dorene clapped her hands. "Take the next exit, Whelper."

"Jesus, girl," Buddy said, holding his ear where he still felt the air-whizz of the wrench zipping past. He looked over at her. She was brushing damp tendrils of hair off her face. She looked wispy and beautiful. Buddy thought of Faye Dunaway in *Bonnie and*

Clyde, and he wondered, with clammy dismay, who the hell that made him.

All the way back to his place, Buddy kept looking in the rearview for the car, but it didn't follow after that, couldn't, he knew. Still he kept his eyes peeled. He and Dorene were silent most of the way until she said, "So that was a pretty fair introduction to Chad Delmonte. The driver was his friend Garnet Wilson. A real asshole. A cop. He's got one of those army buzz cuts with the shaved temples, white sidewalls they call it in the forces. You can tell he's a bastard just by looking at him. He's a bodybuilder too, wears a size forty-four jacket and thirty-inch-waist pants. I know because Chad was always strutting in front of the bathroom mirror, flexing his biceps to compare. Garnet developed his stomach muscles to where he could stand with his arms akimbo and roll them in waves. Chad treated him like that made him some goddamn superhero. Mr. Universe."

As soon as they got inside Buddy's apartment, Dorene said, "You better pack, Whelper. We can't stay here. Garnet would have taken down our license plate for sure. He'll come after us sooner than later."

Then she stared at Buddy directly, fixed her gaze upon him and held it without wavering. He knew she was thinking that now he had a choice. He didn't have to go with her, and she was wondering what choice he would make. He could say: see you later, two wrongs don't make a right, thanks but no thanks. Get himself out while the getting was good. He ought to have, he knew. But instead he reached under the bed and pulled out his suitcase, laid it open on the mattress.

Dorene smiled with relief. She put her fingertips to his cheek, kissed his mouth softly. "Angel," she said, her lips fluttering against his.

Buddy packed his clothes and toiletries and papier-mâché project, which whether he went to class or not was still required to be done in three weeks if he intended to move up to the next, final level: Expert Master.

"What about Leonard?" Dorene said. The parrot was in its cage, chewing a small rawhide bone Dorene had taken from Rhoda's apartment. It had a black tongue and perked on hearing its name. "Go ahead, make my day," it said.

"Pack him," Buddy replied.

In less than an hour, they were loaded into the Hair Pins' minibus and on the highway, heading west. Buddy felt guilty about taking the bus, and he knew, unless he was dead lucky, no good could come of it. It was almost 2 A.M., and after a while, Dorene leaned her head back and went to sleep. Buddy shot the Ford up to seventy and drove, trying not to think too much about to where, catching a dose of road fever that made him care less anyway.

SEVENTEEN

WHEN HE was too tired to drive anymore, Buddy pulled into the parking lot of a Heritage Motor Inn. The rooms spread out along a covered verandah overlooking a lawn with twin oaks and a tiny, unfilled, concrete swimming pool. Beside each door was a metal chair with a scallop-shaped back. Next to the office, on a twenty-foot stand, was a revolving neon sign that thrummed with the sound of coursing neon gas and spelled out VACANCY/AIR-CONDITIONED/POOL/CABLE TV all in green and pink beneath a blinking yellow arrow. Buddy got them a room at the back where he could park right in front of the door. He roused Dorene and she stumbled inside like a sleepwalker, climbing into the bed without saying boo, asleep before her head hit the pillow. Buddy brought all their stuff in, taking trips back and forth, since even covered under the tarp, he didn't think it prudent to leave everything unsecured the whole rest of the night. To his relief, the parrot seemed none the worse for wear when Buddy unwrapped the wool blankets from its cage to check it, and he guessed it had been amply protected from the wind speed and chill by Dorene's thoughtfulness.

In the morning, what woke them was a pert tap on the door and a key sliding into the lock and turning, the door bump-stopping against the chain Buddy had connected as an afterthought, getting out of bed especially, when he'd found his mind racing too fast to sleep.

"Oops," a woman's voice chirped. Then, "I don't know what's wrong with the Do Not Disturb signs that people don't care to use them. All these locks and chains. I for one am sick of trying to open doors that cannot be opened." The door banged shut.

"Just the maid," Buddy said out loud, as much to reassure himself as Dorene.

"Scared me, though," Dorene said. "Who was she talking to?"

Dorene got up and went into the bathroom, and Buddy could see her through the doorway from where he lay on the bed, standing in front of the sink, splashing water onto her face then drying it with a little handtowel. He looked away when she sat down on the toilet.

"I'm starving, Whelper, how about you?"

"I could eat," he told her. After he heard the toilet flush, he watched her tease her hair in front of the mirror, tying it into a knot that brought it up off her shoulders, exposing the delicate nape of her neck in a pretty way. "There's a pancake house right across the road we could grab a bite at."

"Sounds good," Dorene said, coming out of the bathroom and noticing the motel room for the first time—the plaster on the walls, the cracked ceiling, the chipped black headboard on the queen bed.

Buddy saw her take it all in and he felt responsible, like he should explain just what he meant bringing her to such a dump. "I stopped when I got tired," he said lamely. "There was this bright neon sign that caught my eye and an arrow pointing to here. It was a wonderful sign in the dark. You can imagine."

Dorene came and sat down on the bed. "I don't care, Whelper. It's fine. It's such a relief to be out and moving somewhere, I don't give a hoot what it looks like, a hole or a palace, doesn't matter to me. Just so long as the ceiling doesn't fall in on us while we're sleeping." She pulled at the gray chenille bedspread with growing perturbation. "You know, though, they don't hardly ever wash these bedspreads. It's the one thing I do hate about motel rooms: lying under other people's filth and who knows what else—boogers, love juices. For hygienic reasons, you should make a habit of always removing the bedspread and asking for an extra blanket instead when you first check in. Crabs, lice, I'm afraid to think what all we might have caught."

At the pancake house, they sat at a sticky table still damp from being wiped, Buddy ducking his head under an ominous hanging basket containing a drooping mass of ferns. They both ordered blueberry pancakes with whipped cream, and coffee. The coffee was topped up regularly, before it could ever get below the halfway point, so that they had no idea how many full cups they drank during the course of their breakfast. When she was finished eating all of her pancakes and some of Buddy's, which she forked onto her plate with a touch of shame, mumbling something about how after all those instant breakfasts real food was a treat, Dorene took a stack of envelopes out of her purse.

"My mail," she said. "It was in a pile on the kitchen counter at Chad's, neat as you please. It's a wonder Gloria didn't snoop through it already. Or maybe she did and glued everything shut again to cover her tracks. She's such a degenerate." Dorene slit open the envelopes with her thumbnail and then read the contents earnestly—bills, junk mail—each by each, slowly and with changing expressions. Buddy excused himself to the washroom to give her privacy and to hunt for a toothpick. When he came back Dorene was practically jumping out of her seat with excitement.

"Guess what?" she said as soon as he'd ducked the ferns and sat down. She was waving a letter in front of his face. "We're going to Memphis! Our timing couldn't be better if we'd tried. This is the one hope I had, and almost lost, now it looks like it's going to pan out. Listen to this." And she read to Buddy the letter inviting her to audition for the position of backup singer to Macon Wells, a country-blues sensation, apparently, whom Buddy had never heard of, which provoked Dorene to cluck her tongue and frown at him rather harshly. They liked the tape she'd sent and wondered could she make it to Memphis to try out, since they were actively seeking to replace one of their singers—Macon always had three backing him—who had joined a religious commune after stopping to chat with a by-all-accounts sexy Moonie she'd run into at the airport on their way back from a gig in Chicago. Their attempts to rescue and deprogram her had failed. They were sad about that. Macon just wanted to make music, and with a five-state tour coming up, he was anxious to get started rehearsing. They looked forward to hearing Dorene sing both solo and backup to Mr. Wells, changing her wardrobe, if she didn't mind, maximum twice during the audition. They wished her luck.

"What they don't know, Whelper, is that luck is no stranger to me lately. Once I would say my luck was only hard. I had only hard luck. Then I met you. It's no fluke we managed to shake off Garnet Wilson and Chad. I just know I'll get the job. Watch see if I don't. I audition in four days." She smiled at Buddy, radiant. "Honestly, I'm so grateful to you," she said through lovely, bright eyes.

Dorene reached for his hand and squeezed it across the table. She was almost vibrating, Buddy thought, thrumming like the neon sign that had beckoned him the night before, as though she herself might glow in the dark, illuminating the space around her for some far distance. And Buddy knew that if Dorene was a flame burning, he was a moth, helpless to resist the marvelous light, drawing close and retreating, drawing close at his own peril.

Buddy paid for the pancakes while Dorene put away her mail, then they walked back to their motel room to load up and go. They'd be heading north now as well as west, but at least they'd started out somewhat in the right direction. They would probably hit Memphis in about six hours, Buddy figured, taking into account stopping for lunch and filling the tank with gas.

The maid was in the room when they got there. She was playing on the floor with Leonard. She had a face cloth folded around her finger, where the bird had bitten her, and fresh blood was seeping through. It looked pretty bad.

"Don't worry," she said, seeing both their alarmed faces. "It's my fault for taking him out of his cage so soon, before he'd gotten used to me. I love parrots. My brother had one when we were growing up but it got struck by lightning in the backyard just before he left for the navy. This one's a doll. Bites are normal, self-defense for them. Rhubarb, my brother's parrot, actually chomped two of my father's fingers down to the bone in the years we had him. They're kind of like feathered pit bulls when they care to be. From what I understand, most of them like women better than men anyhow because our voices are more tuneful. Rhubarb admired pretty women. He'd wolf whistle whenever he spotted one. 'Yo, Mama!' he'd say. He was macho. You should have heard him if he ever caught me naked. I mean, it was embarrassing being ogled and whistled at by a parrot. He was right to hate my father, though."

The maid reached for the cigarette she'd left smoldering on the edge of the dresser. "You caught me. We're not supposed to smoke in the rooms. I could get fired over this, if you tell."

"We won't tell, hon, but you've got to give me a drag. I quit by accident. I keep trying to recall those gory pictures of smokers' lungs, but I don't care. I don't care what my lungs look like inside, or what that says about my views on health practices." Dorene took the cigarette into the bathroom with her.

The maid looked at Buddy. "You won't tell either?" she said.

Buddy shook his head.

"Swear?"

Buddy swore.

"I trust you." She stroked between Leonard's eyes and put him back in his cage. "It's hard to believe that parrots need the same balanced diet people need. My brother used to let me help him when he'd make Rhubarb's parrot ball—his favorite food. We'd roll three different kinds of beans, corn, rice, dog food, garlic, Oxo and seasonings for flavor into a ball the size of a fist. Rhubarb loved my brother. He'd sit on his shoulder for hours, picking through his hair for parasites. I miss them both like crazy." The maid stood to her height of four-foot-nine tops and went about stripping the sheets from the bed.

Dorene called Buddy to come into the bathroom. She was sitting on the rim of the tub, flicking ashes into the toilet. She looked tired under the hard light from the ceiling bulb, and when she put the cigarette to her lips, there were lines Buddy hadn't seen before. "Hey, Whelper, why don't you give that girl Leonard?" she said in a hoarse whisper. "As a present. I know it's your pet and all, but I would. Let's face it, we were thinking more along the lines of a little dog, weren't we? Do you want to be rolling parrot balls the rest of your life? It's up to you, it's just a suggestion." Dorene pitched the cigarette butt into the toilet and its fire went out with a hiss. "Gee, Whelper, you're cute with your hair cut. Come here, babe. Dixie was right, you know. You ought to grow a goatee like Bruce Willis or Charlie Sheen."

Buddy didn't realize that he had Gloria's honey rose lipstick, which Dorene had stolen for herself from Chad's apartment, smeared across his mouth when he offered the maid his pet. She was just putting the bedspread back on the bed when he told her Leonard was up for grabs.

"Are you serious?" she shouted and leapt onto the bed, bouncing like on a trampoline. "I swear I'll keep him inside during storms. This is wild. By the way, mister, that's a nice bag of shrimp you have there, but you want to hustle put it on ice so they don't turn bad."

"Take the shrimps too, if you feel like it," Dorene called from the bathroom.

"Wow," the maid said. "What did I do to deserve this?"

Back on the freeway, Dorene practiced her singing to the radio in between telling Buddy stories about growing up with Destinee Oracle for a mother. Every year on Dorene's birthday, Destinee had put the kind of candles on her cake that don't blow out. Joke candles. Every year Dorene had tried to blow them out anyway, year after year, wishing for once Destinee would see she was blowing her damn hardest, wishing for normal candles. A normal life, a normal mother, candles that blew out and gave you what you wanted.

When Destinee drove any place in her car, she always drove barefoot. She took only routes that permitted her to get from A to B without making lefthand turns, which she found to be nerve-racking, dicey procedures. Also, Destinee would merge only if she absolutely had to, and never drove on the highway if she could help it, or without taking an extra-strength aspirin first.

Every now and then, she'd decide to let all the plants in their house die. Plants were more responsibility than she could handle at the moment, was the only explanation she'd give Dorene at those times when the leaves shriveled into themselves, crumbling to dust for lack of attention.

The sky was the color of tin as Buddy drove, and then finally the rain came on. It stayed with them mile after mile. They stopped for lunch and gas, and as they got into the Great Smoky Mountains of Tennessee, the rain cleared and the sun broke free of the clouds. Heat rose steaming from the damp pavement. At Chattanooga, the mini-bus stalled and Buddy got it going again, but then it stalled and lurched on a ways, stalled and wouldn't hardly accelerate, and Buddy nudged it into a gas station to be fixed. A replacement part had to be ordered so they'd have to hang around a day, waiting. Dorene and Buddy splurged on a room in the Chattanooga Choo-Choo Hilton. There they made love with gusto. Dorene was acrobatic and imaginative, play-acting out the erotic scenarios she made up with breathtaking conviction.

Afterwards, their lips bruised and swollen from kissing, they strolled around downtown through the Southern Railway Terminal where the famed Choo-Choo and other vintage trains were kept, along with some Victorian-era shops and a huge gas-lit restaurant in the station's former lobby. On their way back to the hotel, Dorene licked an ice-cream cone the size of a baby's head. They felt like they were on a happy vacation, limbo-lost, killing time. Except that Dorene bought a pair of blue-mirrored sunglasses and a bottle of strawberry-blond hair dye to change her hair color. Buddy knew she was trying to disguise herself just in case Chad somehow came to find her. She bought flashy platform sandals and a slinky halter top. Buddy paid for everything because he still thought Dorene ought to save her money for Memphis and, who knew what, unforeseen ruts down the road. Especially since she might not be so wrong to fret about Garnet Wilson using his police connections to track them to where they were waiting on a new used fuel pump. Buddy imagined that an APB had gone out across the South, and he bought her roses.

EIGHTEEN

DORENE dyed her hair a sassy shade of blond, peach rather than strawberry-tinted is how it developed, while Buddy slept. She guessed she'd worn him out because that last time he'd practically begged her to go easy on him, he protested he was getting rubbed raw, though mostly it was a pleasurable sensation, he admitted through clamped teeth. She wasn't a sex fiend normally, it was just being on the road to a new life, a great job prospect shining on her horizon, made her horny. She couldn't explain it exactly but she felt light and willing to bend. She couldn't get enough of Buddy.

She'd even felt jealous twinges when she'd asked him about his ex-wife, and he'd told her how he still called her on the phone sometimes. "What for?" Dorene had quizzed him, but now she was thinking about it, she couldn't recall what his answer had been. It was hard to imagine Buddy being married to anybody. He had a loner's aura about him. She couldn't picture him keeping up his side of a breakfast conversation for year upon wedded year. That didn't mean anything, though. Chad was a real smooth-talker and look where it had landed him. Well, almost landed him, if her attempted murder had been successful.

Dorene held her breath and tiptoed over to where Buddy was nestled in the bed. He hadn't even stirred. The feeling she had, looking at him, struck her as both happy and sad combined. He was so handsome now and normal, which she knew was on account of her. Somehow, without even meaning to, really, she'd taken him over, homogenized him. But at least, Dorene comforted herself, she could show Buddy off with pride in Memphis. With her new blond hair, they'd make a cute couple. One day she might even be able to sing to him from a stage, a romantic notion she'd always dreamed of carrying out with a boyfriend. A frown skimmed the surface of her face.

Buddy was right not to have a clue who Macon Wells was. She'd heard of him, vaguely recalled the name, and she thought she might even recognize his music if she heard it. But calling Macon Wells a "sensation" was sugar-coating reality in a way she couldn't bring herself to accept, much as she would have liked for it to be true. Still, there was no predicting that he wouldn't be the next Garth Brooks. The music industry was dramatic—aflower with heartaches and miracles. God, she had high hopes. So high she was giving herself vertigo, picturing herself on top of the world.

Dorene stroked Buddy's cheek with the back of her hand. He smiled in his sleep like an infant. She suddenly felt so lonely. She was her own keeper. Maybe it boiled down to her being a Gemini. She'd read once that Geminis go through life searching for their missing twin, never feeling whole or unabandoned. Dorene's aloneness was so heavy a weight on her that she didn't think her single self could bear it. She wanted Buddy awake. She took hold of his arm and shook it gently.

"Hey," she said. "Are you recuperated yet?" She climbed into the bed beside him. She nuzzled the scratchy hinge of his jaw, still mildly flavored with after-shave. She kissed his flat, rough nipple and smooched her way down his belly. He groaned and at first she took that as encouragement but then she changed her mind, unsure if it wasn't, after all, a groan of disapproval, even pain. She wavered. Should she stop or go on, she wondered? When she tried things that he'd responded to earlier, athletically and eagerly—but didn't respond to now—it dawned on her that he was actually still asleep and she gave it up, feeling slightly perverted. Dorene tried to comfort herself with the friendly warmth of his body against hers, take solace in the kooky itch of his pubic hair tickling her earlobe.

In the morning, they had eggs sunny-side up in the hotel's coffee shop. Dorene was in a bad mood. She had a crick in her neck that forced her to turn her entire upper body if she wanted to look over her shoulder. It amazed her how many times she wanted to do just that. Despite this disability, it was Dorene who first spotted Garnet Wilson flashing his badge at a receptionist behind the front desk. "Fuck," Dorene said, which startled Buddy and caused a posse of little children to break into a machine-gun spray of giggles, drawing attention to them all. Dorene quickly pulled Buddy into the gift shop off the main lobby so they could talk privately, crouched behind a rack of souvenirs. She couldn't figure out how Garnet could have trailed them to Tennessee. It was Buddy who cottoned on to the credit card he'd been using the whole distance. Tears swam in Dorene's eyes.

She knew Garnet was not a man to let things go. To him she was a dumb stripper with delusions of grandeur who'd tried to murder his best friend. Not that he had a clue about the music business, or her delusions either. She had a dim memory of Garnet in a roomful of so-called stags, watching her strip, crushing empty can after can of beer in his fist. He'd had a little puppy with him that he let eat trash scraps and cigarette stubs. Garnet's nose had been broken and reset poorly, but still he resembled Burt Reynolds. After Burt dumped Loni, Garnet complained to Chad that every woman he tried to pick up now hated Burt Reynolds and him too, by default. Garnet and Chad both had violent temperaments, which is probably why they got along. Chad had gone out with Garnet for fun sometimes in his unmarked police car. Cruising around, Garnet would take a leak in a coffee can he kept on the floor for that purpose, but Chad wouldn't do it—there were parts of being a cop Chad disagreed with. He was in awe of Garnet's badge, though. Also the handcuffs, the holstered .38, the sap, the power.

Chad had described the sap to Dorene in detail, since Garnet had let him use it. It was black leather, eight inches long, with a wrist loop at one end, and filled with buckshot. To meet their daily arrest quotas, vice cops often pretended to be gay and hit public rest rooms. A man had fondled Chad's rear end, and Garnet had grabbed the man's wrist and twisted it up behind his back in one motion, jerked the arm higher until it broke at the elbow. The guy had fallen to his knees, and Chad had been given the privilege of clipping him behind the ear with the blackjack. The man had immediately gone unconscious. Chad thought Garnet was showing off when he kicked the supine man in the jaw with the toe of his boot. The jaw had cracked audibly and blood had poured from his nose and mouth. As far as Dorene knew, Garnet had never announced he was a cop or tried to make an arrest. Jesus.

Who were the criminals? Herself? Chad? Garnet? There was a story in all the newspapers about a woman who sliced off her husband's dick after she claimed he raped her. She cut it off and threw it out her car window into a field. The cops searched the field, found the severed organ, and hours later it was reattached through delicate surgery. "Why," they asked her, "did you do it?" Well, why do they think?

"Oh shit, Whelper," Dorene swore. "What am I going to do?" Her hands were clamped over her face. She smelled Chad's cologne before she heard him on the other side of the rack debating with Garnet which souvenir Chattanooga T-shirt to buy. Garnet thought he ought to buy a beer mug but Chad wanted a

T-shirt. After a while, they bought some Cheese Nips and left. The smell of him stayed curled in her nostrils. "That's it for me. Garnet's tracked me like a hound. They're going to make this road trip a party. Catching me will be the most fun they've had since they forced Garnet's little dog to snort cocaine."

But Buddy started speaking in her ear and what he said made sense. Dorene blew her nose and tried to get a grip on herself. "You'd do that?" she said, scrutinizing Buddy the way you would anything too good to be true. She turned what he said over in her mind, examining it like supermarket produce stickered at a price less than its retail value so you didn't want to buy it, pretty sure that when you got it home there'd be a nasty flaw at its core.

"Okay, Whelper. I don't see I have a choice. I got a hard glimpse of my future behind bars, Garnet Wilson abusing his authority. I'm a desperado. I'll do what I have to do to feel the wind in my hair and make my audition. Bye, honey," she said, kissing his mouth hungrily. "I'm going to eat you with a spoon when we meet up again in Memphis. We'll have a triple X-rated reunion, I promise." Dorene put on her blue sunglasses. She took some bills out of her bra and pushed them into Buddy's shirt pocket. "Slink," she told him, "be slippery as an eel and go at least as far as Miami before you U-turn."

NINETEEN

BUDDY charged two Trailways bus tickets to Jackson, Mississippi, on his Visa card. He hoped Garnet would be duped, coaxed by the plastic stool pigeon into following his decoy while he wended down to Miami using the credit card at regular intervals, enabling Dorene to hopefully make a clean getaway driving the mini-bus to Memphis. The Hair Pins would be pretty angry by now, Buddy bet.

He'd left the keys to his pickup under the driver's seat and a note for them on the dash saying he had an emergency and needed to switch vehicles. For the tournament over in Claxton, he hoped they'd drive his pickup. They could help themselves too to the hot VCRs, if the boxes were still there. He knew they'd hate having to seat some of the team like fruit pickers in the open back, since their hair would get wind-mussed. The Hair Pins believed perfect hair was one of their best weapons of intimidation against opposing bowlers.

While he waited at the depot, Buddy bought himself a Pabst Blue Ribbon ballcap, some peppermint Breathsavers and a news magazine he flipped through without spending much effort reading. He was distracted by a kid running back and forth in the aisle between the waiting-room chairs. The kid was making the sound of breaking wind by pumping down on a hand cupped under his armpit. Buddy couldn't tell who he belonged to because nobody wasn't ignoring him. When Buddy unrolled a mint, the kid came and sat down beside him.

"Can I have a candy?" he said to Buddy. "Please," he added, although it didn't sound meant, in fact rang of mockery.

"I don't have any candy, son. These are breath mints for adults," Buddy said. "Don't you know you should never take candy from a stranger?"

"Why?" the kid asked.

"It might be poison."

"Why would a stranger want to poison me?"

"Lots of reasons," Buddy said.

"You just don't want to share," the kid accused, working himself up. "I said the magic word. I asked nicely, but you're not cooperating. You're not friendly."

The kid went back to what he'd been doing before, only this time a pretty woman with black hair told him to stop it or she'd keep the TV off for a week, she'd make him drink his milk without chocolate sprinkles, she'd hold off buying him anything he wanted forever, if he kept being rude and disturbing people. She smiled apologetically at Buddy and he could see in her face how it hurt her to have to threaten her boy that way, especially in public.

"What about making him do chores?" Buddy suggested. "You could make him responsible for cleaning up the yard, raking leaves, mowing the lawn, picking up litter."

"Get out," the kid gasped. "What's the idea trying to ruin my life, mean stranger."

"He's got a good thing going with you," Buddy told the beautiful mother.

She tilted her head to the side. "Possibly. I give him an easy ride, but it might be the last one he gets, right? Anyhow, what you're seeing is nothing. Behind closed doors we're both a lot worse. We do real harm and then feel awful after. Sometimes we have to lie down on the sofa and hold on to each other like castaways. What, Kyle?" The boy whispered in her ear. "Why on earth would he want to poison you? He doesn't even know you." The attractive woman looked at Buddy and embarrassment rose gently between them.

On the bus, Buddy got next to a window at the back. He read. He dozed. In Tuscaloosa, there was a brief stopover while they took on a new driver and refueled. Buddy got out to stretch his legs and use the washroom in the terminal. He dropped change into a vending machine and bought a snack, out of boredom more than hunger, and carried it onto the bus with him. He had some coffee in a paper cup with handles, and a heavy cakelike donut that stuck in his throat. He ate a few bites of it, then tried to cram the rest into the metal ashtray on the back of the seat in front of him.

"Stop that pushing," the woman in front whined. "I felt that like a jab in my kidneys."

In Jackson, Buddy bought a pair of tickets to New Orleans, and then he boarded an older, less comfortable motor coach. He managed to claim for himself a double space at the back near the lavatory so he wouldn't be as cramped. Watching the people go into and out of the toilet in fits and spurts made him introspective, melancholy. Darkness fell and a low white moon ran alongside the bus, just behind the tops of the scraggly pines shouldering the highway. Buddy had his head wedged in against the seat and the window, using his ballcap as a pillow. The bus swerved to avoid something in the road, a dead animal probably, but then bumped across it anyway. Buddy's head clabbered against the window glass and he swore under his breath. A while later, the diesel engine changed pitch and the brakes moaned and hissed as the bus pulled up at a rest station. Buddy didn't get off this time, although others did, irritating those passengers who had finally gotten themselves to sleep sitting upright.

Buddy was making a run for it in his mind. He thought that his reason had broken down and desire had taken him over. But was that true? Had his reason broken down or had it broken out? He knew he was free to do what he pleased with his life. He could live it alone or joined up with somebody else, the choice was his. The problem was, while he was most comfortable being on his own, the kind of *un*comfortable he felt when he was around a woman—around Dorene—was so exquisite, such honey-sweet torture, that once he felt it, he couldn't give it up. He feared he'd be dull and unsensational without it. He felt a crush of tenderness for Dorene. Buddy wished he could make love to her here on the bus, touch her under cover of his jacket. It was sick, he decided, masochistic, since what he wanted, really, was to be left alone, his thoughts clear and unsullied by longing. He didn't want to live dramatically. He didn't appreciate being given a leading role in a soap opera. But there it was. He was a prisoner of desire. Passion had taken him hostage. A fire had ignited his blood and he was burning. He'd be burned, he knew. All he could resolve was to keep a bucket of cold common sense nearby. He'd douse himself when he became desperate for his own company, and let passion roll off his back like rain in a starless night.

Just as the bus started to leave, somebody came running up alongside, pounding on the metal flanks end to front, the length of the bus. The driver swung open the doors. An out-of-breath woman hoisted herself up the stairs, carrying a shopping bag with stuff escaping out of it, an appliance's electrical cord dangled loose. Buddy stood up in a kind of crouch and tried to indicate that he had a good place to sit at the back. The woman came listing down the aisle, bumping people with her shopping bag, and stopped at Buddy, who stowed her loot in the overhead rack while she took the window seat.

"I thought for certain I'd miss the bus," she said. "I got talking inside and forgot what time it was. It stinks back here by the toilet."

"You get used to it," Buddy said.

"*You* might," the woman said.

The conversation got easier later. The woman, whose name was CeCe, was on a quest to find her birth mother. She'd left behind her two little kids and her husband, a fortune teller who went by Sherman the Uncanny, though she'd never called him that. She was going to send each of her family their own picture postcard when she got to New Orleans, but already she confessed she didn't know if she'd be able to find postcards appropriate for little kids, with animals or Disney characters.

"Everywhere I go you wouldn't believe the hard time I have. Check for yourself if they're not all either scenic overviews of the place taken from a helicopter, or naughty cartoons with sexual quips in balloons. Postcard manufacturers don't consider that a mama might be off on her own exploring and need to send her kids a hello note, with Xs and Os at the end to tell them she was hugging and kissing them in her mind and they should try to imagine it too, that she would miss her children and not always be near a phone. I guess they figure kids can't read postcards, but who do they think is looking after them? A moron? Children can't cook either, or wash their own hair. I mean, who in their right mind would leave their babies with somebody who couldn't read them a postcard their mama sent? I swear, if I wasn't spending so much time hunting for adorable postcards, I'd be sipping tea in my biological mother's living room by now."

Buddy couldn't see the woman's face clearly in the half light of the bus as it drove on down the moon-drenched road, but after a while she seemed to prefer staring at her own reflection in the window over talking with him, so he kept quiet. He imagined she had private conversations going on in her head he should keep out of, planning what she would say to her mother when, and if, she finally found her and they could look each other over through soggy eyes, view for themselves the superb wonder of genetics.

In New Orleans, Buddy boarded a bus to Jacksonville, Florida, and as it backed out of the dock, he waved bye to CeCe with one finger. She stood watching him but she didn't wave. For a long time on the new bus, Buddy wondered why she didn't wave back. He decided she was not into good-byes, having left behind her kids and husband to go searching for the biggest hello of her life. Hello not good-bye was what she cared for. If he'd been coming and not going, and she knew him, it would have been a different story. He bet she would have waved then. Buddy contemplated why he was thinking about CeCe at all and not Dorene and not what the hell he was doing taking a billion buses to Miami. He drove the thought to the end of the road but met a dead end. He figured he was caught up in a windstorm. He was being blown fast and furious, any place as good as the next until things died down. He tried to tell himself his life would be his own again, Dorene but a gust in his long-range forecast. He could spare some time to fall in love with her. He could afford, and truly ought, to throw her a line to save her from spinning out of control on a tornado of trouble. He would tether her, delicately, until she was ready to stand upright again. Just so long as she didn't pull him off his feet, the weight of them both together more than he could handle on his own.

At a rest stop somewhere, he relieved himself and then put change into a pay phone and dialed his ex-wife's number. It rang a long time, longer than usual because he knew Cheryl kept the phone on her night table. Sometimes she picked up even before he'd heard the first ring on his side.

"Hello?"

"Cheryl?" Buddy asked, hopelessly, because it was a man.

"I don't think so."

"It must be Toomer then," Buddy said in what he remembered as his car salesman's voice. "This is Buddy Whelper, Cheryl's ex."

"So? She's not here," Toomer said. "She's out of town on business. Why do you keep pestering her? You call and then you don't say anything. There's no point to that. This is the middle of the night. You should be sleeping."

"I can't," Buddy said.

"Why don't you watch TV then? All evening they've been promoting the late, late movie. It's a good one—*The Karate Kid*—I can recommend it. Why don't you watch that until you can sleep?"

"I saw it already. In the theater."

"Watch it again on TV."

"There's no TV where I am," Buddy hated to admit.

"I guess I can't help you then."

"Guess not."

"I'm going to hang up now."

"Nice talking with you, Toomer," Buddy said. "Oh, hey—did those leeches do the trick?" One thing, Toomer said good-bye the same way Cheryl did, letting the dial tone say it for him.

The bus reached Jacksonville in the very early morning. The sun was not hot yet but it was bright and painful to Buddy's grainy eyes. In the station, he bought a plastic razor, some shaving foam, a toothbrush and mouthwash, aviator sunglasses, and charged it all on his Visa. He groomed in the washroom, and though he couldn't do anything about the mauve circles under his eyes, he felt better when he emerged some time later. In the coffee shop he ordered a country-style breakfast, which came with everything he'd ever considered eating in the morning, piled on the same plate, plus his own thermos of coffee to wash it down. A final bus would take him to Miami but it didn't leave for two hours, so he lingered over his food. When the waitress came and told him he was entitled to more, to all he could eat, he laughed and patted his gut. He was busting at the seams already, he told her, he wouldn't need to eat again for a week as it was.

"Then you just threw your money down the drain. Picky eaters shouldn't order all-you-can-eat. You ought to have ordered a regular breakfast for a regular appetite, eggs, bacon, sausage, grits, hash browns, stewed tomato, if you weren't all that hungry. Well, live and learn. Now you know. I'm going to bring you some more coffee, at least. You have room for that?"

Buddy used a pay phone to call Cosmo. When Cosmo's answering machine clicked on, Buddy hung up. How was he going to explain what he didn't understand himself? Where was he headed and why? What did love have to do with it? He'd met a damsel in distress and she had him wrapped around her baby finger. Her cries for help had led him into deep water, and he'd gone willingly for the most part. He'd waded in up to his shoulders before he'd thought twice about drowning. He called Cosmo again and said he was sorry for the short notice and inconvenience but he'd gone on vacation for a while. Since Buddy had covered for him with the Hair Pins, he hoped Cosmo wouldn't mind taking a turn filling in as super. Buddy was choosing to overlook the fact that he'd subbed for just one night as bowling coach, and he expected Cosmo to act as super for, truthfully, he couldn't speculate how long. He said he'd return the mini-bus as soon as he could, with its almost-new fuel pump, and hoped nobody had bothered to call the police.

Near Vero Beach, Buddy delivered a baby. Actually all he did was catch it and hold on, no small feat, slick and slippery as it was, to prevent it rolling on the ground and getting dirty.

The mother-to-be had started wailing low, shifting in her seat and then leaking a large amount of water, which she felt embarrassed about but couldn't help, of course. Buddy told her it was natural, he guessed, and there were lots of paper towels on hand. The driver had stopped the bus when it became clear they wouldn't make it to any hospital in time, and Buddy had collected donations of extra clothes from the passengers so he could make a little bed on the grass next to the highway.

He was surprised that the woman didn't want to lie down. Not at all, until nearly the end. Instead she paced back and forth, crutching on Buddy for support, swearing at her absent husband when she had the breath to. The people on the bus got out and sat around on the grass as though they were at a picnic. Some of them watched the woman for entertainment, others didn't seem to notice her deliberately or by chance, which is a common range of reaction a crowd will show to a spectacle, Buddy guessed. He kept checking over his shoulder, looking down the road for Chad and Garnet. The delay might let them close the gap.

When the woman did choose to lie down, she didn't really lie down. At first she squatted. Then she got on her hands and knees like a cat. Then she asked Buddy to pull off her underpants while she lay back, propped on her elbows. She spread her knees apart and pushed. Buddy stopped checking over his shoulder when she stranded the baby with its head half in, half out of her and screamed that she was not going to push anymore because it was torture, it was killing her, ripping her in two. It did look gruesome. Buddy didn't like the way the infant's skull was being clamped in a vise grip, and he urged its mother, please, to get it out. Maybe it was what he said or probably the woman realized she couldn't leave things the way they were, she was all body, she couldn't separate herself from it. She reminded Buddy of an animal with its leg caught in a trap. Either it had to gnaw off its own foot and free itself to hobble away, or it would remain trapped and die slowly. There was no happy choice. The woman began pushing again with all the fury she could muster. Pretty soon the baby's head was out, and enough of a shoulder that Buddy could do some twisting and tugging and pry loose the upper body, which then uncorked the rest so it slipped out fluidly.

The mother held the newborn girl on her chest, clearing goop out of its nose and mouth with her finger until it started mewling, which seemed to relieve her. But then about ten minutes later, the woman started panting again and bearing down. Twins, Buddy thought. He put out his hands just as a bloody mess splatted out from her, which he tried his best to catch. He caught some. He turned the main bulk of tissue over in his hands but there was no head or legs or baby parts he could identify, it was more like a heart or a spleen, or a lung. He held up the mess for the mother to see, like something from a horror movie.

"Afterbirth," she panted at him. "Garbage. Drop it."

"Garbage?" Buddy said. He didn't know about afterbirth, he'd never heard about afterbirth, but he trusted the woman to know her business and he laid the blob down on the grass, carefully though, since it was still connected to her first baby by the cord. He wiped his hands on somebody's donated jacket.

An ambulance came along, with a newspaper crew following behind, and a photographer took their picture. A reporter asked the woman what she was going to name her baby. You could tell he was disappointed when she said Daisy Lee, and not Vero Beach or Trailways or something more newsworthy to print. Buddy held the just-born girl wrapped in a soft flannel blanket while the woman was sewn with needle and thread, stitched to close where her flesh had given, delivering her child's perfect head into the round sunshine.

It was after midnight before Buddy checked into a hotel on the oceanfront strip in Miami Beach. The Sea Breeze on Collins Avenue boasted attractive nautical Scandinavian decor and carpeted rooms. Though he was tired, Buddy wanted to feel sand cool between his toes, wade his feet in the ocean. When he got down to the shore, he stood in the surf, surveying a rare, dazzling phosphorescence in the tide. He took a step and scattered sparks. It was magical. The water was luminous, ultraviolet. When he walked through it, phosphorescence clung to the hair on his legs. He splashed water with his hands and it glittered sequins. Buddy dove into the glowing shoals, belly-flopping like Daisy Lee into the brilliant light, holding his breath.

TWENTY

DORENE crossed the parking lot at Sears, digging in her purse for her keys to the mini-bus. She'd rented a spacious two-bedroom apartment with a deck, off Beale Street in Memphis, where W.C. Handy blew the first lonesome notes and became the "Father of the Blues." There was a park called Handy Park where she'd sat, nicely shaded by Handy's statue, eating a hero sandwich and drinking an icy Tab while she made up her mind which of the apartments she'd looked at she was going to take.

The one she chose came furnished, but still there were some finishing touches she wanted to get for it—decorative placemats, and clay flowerpots for the kitchen window sill being examples, and why Dorene was at Sears. Though she hadn't found the exact items she was after, she'd pounced on a red Lycra dress on the clearance rack that would be perfect for her Macon Wells audition. Just so long as she could get the stain off the front of it. She'd convinced the floor manager to reduce the price even lower by hemming and hawing as to whether Spray 'n Wash would remove the mark, and then agreeing to let the bill be stamped "Final Sale—No Refunds or Exchanges" and take her chances. If the stain didn't come out, Dorene would be stuck wearing a brooch in an unstrategic spot on her boob.

"Excuse me?"

"What?" Dorene snapped, annoyed she couldn't seem to locate the keys anywhere in her bottomless purse, wondering if she'd left them in the ignition. She tried to shrug off the finger that was tapping her shoulder persistently.

"Haven't you forgotten something?"

"Like what?" Dorene looked up from her purse, and then up into the troubled face of a very tall black man holding a walkie-talkie.

"Isn't there something you've forgotten to pay for, ma'am?"

"I beg your pardon? I bought a red dress, if you must know, though I don't see how it can be any of your business, with a stain that I'm counting on being makeup base and not something stubborn that won't wash out when I get home. I paid cash fair and square. It was a bargain but it won't look cheap when I'm done accessorizing it. Satisfied? Now buzz off."

The man showed Dorene his Sears security badge and told her the store was electronically monitored with tiny television cameras. "Big deal," she said, until he told her he'd seen her on one of his screens stashing tubes of Maybelline lipstick in her pocket. She'd left the store without paying for them, which was shoplifting, and Sears prosecuted its shoplifters.

Dorene fished inside her shorts pocket and pulled out three tubes of lipstick.

"You mean these?" she said, dumping them into the man's hands. "Here, you can have them back. I forgot them was all. I wanted to get some red lipstick to go with my new dress and so I was looking at a bunch of different shades and I guess when I couldn't hold them all, I put some in my pocket without thinking. I don't even want them. I'm going to make do with the honey rose frost I already have. I don't know if I like being spied on, by the way, Big Brother. I might file a complaint. I don't think it's ethical—high-tech peeping toms—what next?"

"Come inside, please, to the security office."

"I didn't mean now. I haven't made up my mind yet. If I decide any of my rights have been violated, I'll file a complaint later. At my convenience."

"You're not understanding me, ma'am. You were caught shoplifting. You'll have to come inside."

"Oh, honestly. Is this 'Candid Camera'?" Dorene said, looking around vaguely. She wasn't feeling well. Her head was pounding with a stress migraine. Everywhere she looked she saw Chad Delmonte clones and it was making her crazy. Dead or alive, she couldn't be rid of him. "I told you it was a mistake. Read my lips: I hate those colors, they don't match my dress. I gave them back, now get lost. I'm going home to scrub out this stain if humanly possible."

"It's the law, ma'am. I have to insist you follow me to the security office. We'll discuss your charges in there."

"I'd rather not."

"You don't have a choice, lady. You were caught shoplifting. Read *my* lips. It's a criminal offense. The police are on their way. Now come with me." The man took hold of Dorene's arm and started leading her back across the parking lot towards the store's big glass doors.

"Take your mitts off me," Dorene said. "I can walk. The police will only laugh at you," she tried, once they got inside, panic rising in her. The police. What if Garnet had put out an APB? This was it. She was caught, her crime spree finito. Well, not without a fight, Dorene thought. She had a big audition tomorrow, her real life waiting just a slow ballad away. "You can't call the police over three stupid lipsticks that I returned. Still safety sealed, I might add. This is dumb, now let me go. I should have called the police on you, told them you were selling soiled merchandise and crappy placemats. When they come, don't be surprised if I'm not the one they arrest."

"Just relax," the man said. "You're making this harder than it has to be."

Walking down the aisles past the racks and shelves of goods, Dorene felt people's eyes on her, and her cheeks flushed with shame, though she insisted to herself she'd done nothing wrong, not intentionally. When they finally got to the security office, it was actually a relief, since at least it was private.

"Listen here, buster," she told the man, leaning forward to get in his face. "Understand: I didn't *steal* the lipsticks, I put them in my pocket by accident and forgot about them. Comprendo? My problem is my hands aren't big enough to hold six tubes of lipstick at once. My mother has even smaller hands and I bet you wouldn't pull this stunt on her. Give me a break. Don't you have something better to do? Where are the police anyway? I thought you said you called the cops." Maybe he'd been bluffing, since it was silly over ten dollars' worth of stuff.

"They'll be here. Have a seat. Calm down, your skin's getting blotchy."

"Don't you dare notice my complexion," Dorene warned.

The room was muggy and stank of coffee, cigarettes and donuts. Two other plainclothes security personnel were watching television monitors, ignoring Dorene except to snicker occasionally between themselves, at her expense is how she took it. Their attention was rooted on a youth in the toy department hovering near the Nintendo display—suspiciously—he even looked it to Dorene. They were just waiting for him to steal something, almost willing him to. It was so unfair. Why couldn't she make it clear she was not like that kid? She sniffed and wiped the beads of sweat off her upper lip. She had honestly made a mistake. She'd made a lot of mistakes, a whole lot, but she was trying to make it right. She did have to question, though, if she didn't have criminal tendencies beyond her control.

The man who'd brought her in was trying out different pens,

checking for ink, until he found one that he then used to fill in her answers to the questions on a sheet he'd pulled off a pad. Her name? She ditched him an alias. Her address? She skewed it slightly. The longer they sat there, the more confident Dorene became that the police weren't coming, had never been called at all, not over bottom-of-the-line lipsticks, and she was merely being intimidated by Sears security into never stealing any more beauty supplies, which she hadn't *stolen* in the first place if anybody bothered to believe what she was telling them in plain English. Anyway, there was always the good chance that Garnet was acting on his own, outside the law, with Chad as his sidekick. She didn't think they could have any hard proof she'd tried to kill her ex-boyfriend—accidents happen.

"Are we almost done?" Dorene said. "I have to go home and feed a sick baby. Plus, I'm behind in my Bible studies."

The man looked at Dorene for a long time with a grave expression. He even put his pen down, trying to make her feel, she understood, the depth of her crime, the steely arm muscle of the justice system when it was flexed, but Dorene just return-stared him, bugging her eyes out like a brat. She knew the police definitely weren't coming or they'd have been there by now. When the man asked to see how much money she had in her purse to write down on his report, she laid a thousand dollars in crumpled bills on his desk.

"See," Dorene said, triumphantly. "Why would I want to steal a bunch of lousy Maybelline lipsticks? I hope you're sorry. You can apologize any time. Go ahead, I'm waiting."

"Listen, lady. People are disturbed. They shoplift for kicks, for the thrill of getting something for nothing. Millionaires' daughters and big-name movie stars shoplift. It can be debilitating, an illness like gambling, or bingeing and purging."

"Well, la de da," Dorene said, because it was the first thing that came to her mind, though it didn't necessarily apply. Her head was throbbing so much it hurt to blink.

"Step onto the painted footprints, please."

Dorene had her photo taken, a mug shot that would stay on record in the security office in case she ever got caught stealing again, at which point worse things would happen to her than being herded through a store full of smug, onlooking customers.

"That's it, I guess," the man said. "You can go."

"Oh, but what about the police?" Dorene said to irritate him.

The man frowned and lit a cigarette, which Dorene could taste, she wanted it so badly. "Theft is not a joke, you know," he said. "Nobody in here laughs about theft. Every year this store alone loses a fortune."

"No wonder," Dorene said, and again she didn't know what she meant by it, just hoped it sounded nasty.

The man shrugged. "Sticks and stones," he said.

Before she left, Dorene offered to take the lipsticks back to the shelf where she'd got them, since she had to pass right by there on her way out to the parking lot. The man declined, looking at her as though she must think he was wet behind the ears.

"Oh, for pete's sake," Dorene huffed, "you wouldn't know a kleptomaniac if you fell over one." And she walked out, shooting the bird to every security camera she passed, her heart pounding, though, despite the tough front. That had been too close.

When she got into the mini-bus, she closed the door and locked it. She cried for half an hour with her head down on the steering wheel before she felt able to drive to her new apartment. She hated feeling like a criminal—being a criminal—whether she set about being one willingly or ended up one by mistake. In truth, she was sorry. Sorry for herself, and Buddy, and Rhoda, and even Chad a little. Sorry for every human creature in the world, troubled seekers all, who just wanted what they wanted and didn't ever mean to hurt anybody trying to get it, but damn well did anyway.

Dorene scooped another spoonful of strawberry Häagen-Dazs

into her mouth direct from the carton. She didn't like living on her own. She was prone to depressing mood swings. What she needed was to keep her hands busy and her mind occupied. After her audition tomorrow she hoped that everything would be different. She'd be on her way, glory-bound, if she got the job. She honestly didn't see why she wouldn't, and that thought injected some cheer into her gloomscape, enough to get her moving down to the newspaper box on the street below, where she put in change for a paper and cleaned it out.

Back upstairs, she set Buddy's pigasus on the kitchen table. She prepared the paste and started ripping the newspapers into inch-wide strips. She ripped Buddy in half before she realized what she'd done and that she held his head and shoulders in one hand, the rest of his body in her other. She pieced the photograph back together and saw Buddy kneeling on some grass at the side of the highway, next to a woman and her newborn baby, whom, apparently, he'd helped deliver. It was a human-interest story. The caption didn't tell Dorene much, except what she already knew. Buddy was a good guy; to put it simply, he was a beaut. She missed him. Then Dorene pulled out a chair and collapsed down into it. She brought the picture up close, squinting into the grainy newsprint.

No doubt. That was Chad and Garnet Wilson beside him. They were looming in the background, caught cracking open cans of beer, them both sitting on the hood of Garnet's car. A mangy dog was adrift in the weeds next to the road. Dorene shivered. Buddy looked so innocent, a sweet samaritan, and there, lurking behind him, thanks to her, was trouble. She felt so powerless to help him—which is how Chad always made her feel. Powerless. Though she really was glad he wasn't dead and that she wasn't a murderer, she couldn't abide that Chad Delmonte would be skulking in her background the rest of her life. She just wanted him to keep the hell away from her. At least, she'd done now what she should have done from the start, which was to put long distance between them physically. Emotionally too, she was working on. There he was, shining like a fancy hood ornament on Garnet's car, a pretty bobble of a man she once did her best to love. God, she hoped Buddy could fend for himself. Dorene took some scissors and carefully cut him out, separate from the picture. Lord knows, she was just trying to take care of herself, live in self-defense. She thought about putting the picture of Buddy in her mouth and swallowing it for safekeeping, but honestly, she didn't want to chance making herself sick before her Macon Wells audition, so she put it in her pocket, hoping some voodoo would protect him. She buried Chad and Garnet in the trash and closed the lid on them.

In the nightclub the next day, once her vision adjusted to the dim light, Dorene teetered, as confidently as she could, on her new stiletto heels past the chairs upside down on the tables, her tight red dress clinging to the tops of her thighs like it was painted on, requiring baby steps to where the band was jamming on a small platform. When the music stopped, she cleared her throat. Macon Wells came to the edge of the platform and checked her out. His drug-glazed eyes settled on the front of her dress. "Nice brooch," he said.

"You know it," Dorene replied.

He held out his hand and helped her up onto the stage. "Ready?" he said, blinding her with a devastating smile.

"Believe it," Dorene said.

TWENTY-ONE

BUDDY ARRIVED in Memphis with a black eye, a split lip, the cap missing off his front tooth and no pubic hair, thanks to Chad and Garnet, who had ambushed him in his hotel room and taken turns pounding him while the other fixed him in a hold so he couldn't fight back. He still had a bruise on the top of his thigh the size and shape of a football where Garnet had slapped his leg with a blackjack. That had been the worst—except for thinking, when the razor was hovering, that he might lose his balls truly, instead of just feeling like he had. The pain from the blackjack had made his entire leg go numb and caused him to vomit. All in all, though, they'd tired of it pretty fast when they hadn't found a trace of Dorene or gotten him to snitch her whereabouts.

Thinking about it after, lying ragged on the floor, pouring Jim Beam down his gullet, Buddy wished he'd been a less passive victim, more of a hero, and taken some forceful action to make them leave Dorene alone, instead of just letting himself get beaten to a pulp. Not that he'd been given a choice, and, either way, it had done the trick. The main thing was, Chad and Garnet had worked revenge out of their systems. All they'd wanted, it seemed, was to even the score, violently. Shaving his groin had been a cruel act of humiliation that went a long way towards making them feel better about the situation with Dorene and the VCRS stolen from

Chad's apartment. In the end, they'd resorted to making crude comments about her that Buddy hadn't liked to hear, and pushing a lamp through his television screen. They'd pissed on the wall, on the floor, on him, and seemed content to close the file on Dorene LaTisha Perney. They'd booted out, leaving Buddy to drift off, hurt and bleeding, on a swirling-sick ride.

Dorene was upset, overcome with pity, when she saw the shape he was in. She pampered him with antiseptic lotions, ice packs and sensual massages meant to rev up his blood and speed healing. The massages hurt, but they seemed to relax Dorene and give her something useful she could do with her hands. She liked the goatee Buddy had grown to surprise her, but his naked private parts were another matter. She was shocked to see his manhood deprived of hair, patchy, scabby where he'd been badly nicked. She could hardly look at his exposed anatomy at all and, when she did bring herself to, she'd either almost cry because she was sorry for him or stare in repugnant wonder until the sight grew so funny she had to laugh. Buddy became adept at keeping himself firmly in the dark.

Dorene was distracted too. Buddy had been in Memphis for a week before she finally got the call she'd been waiting for. She had the job singing backup to Macon Wells. During that week, though, she'd slept fitfully and been restless, hounded by her own demons. She ran hot and cold. At times she'd turn so sullen and mean-tempered that all Buddy could do was keep out of her way and treat her with kid gloves. Other times it was like she couldn't get enough of him. She'd sing his praises so convincingly that they both took heart and ended up in a wild tangle of bedsheets, making sparks. But the truth was, that more and more Dorene was cool towards him, disinterested, remote. Buddy was beginning to see that through the smoky haze of passion, a real fire was smoldering and it might not be such a good thing.

Rehearsals were postponed while the bass guitarist underwent surgery to remove a clump of polyps and kick his drug addiction.

At first, Dorene went around with a rapt smile and seemed almost happy just knowing she would soon be paid to sing and lead the kind of life she'd always dreamed of. Her days passed watching music videos on MTV for inspiration, preening her appearance, eating the meals Buddy cooked for them. But then she grew dissatisfied again, cranky.

Buddy would be sitting at the dinner table squirming, doing pushups from his chair.

"What's wrong with you?" she'd snap.

"Nothing."

"You keep doing things."

"It itches down there. The hair's growing back and it feels like poison ivy. I'm trying not to scratch."

She'd shove her chair back from the table abruptly and go take an endless bath.

She bought a little orange cat with white feet and when she wasn't watching rock videos she sat on the floor teaching it tricks like how to fetch. She'd crumple aluminum foil into a shiny ball and toss it over her head towards the windows at the back of the apartment. The cat would shoot after it, pick up the foil in its mouth and drop it at Dorene's feet. Buddy told himself it was not smart for them to be together from dawn till dark every day, and he took a job repairing bicycles at a sports store where all the clerks wore T-shirts that advised "Get A Wheel Life."

After rehearsals started, Macon Wells began dropping by to pick Dorene up and lingering for a shot of tequila before they went out to practice. He was too tall and skinny, a beanpole of a guy, and kept his fingernails long so he could play his guitar without a pick. He didn't seem at all interested in the dynamics of Buddy and Dorene's relationship. His parents had been hippies and he'd grown up in the back of a van, drinking fresh water from streams, bathing in rivers, shitting in the woods. It irked Buddy that Macon never got his name right.

"So, Bubba," he'd say, "do you eat meat? I'm a vegan." Dorene didn't help.

"Billy," Macon would say, "there's no shame in being a lacto-ovo-vegetarian, either." Dorene let him take all kinds of wild stabs at it, and only eyed both men with a distant, bemused smile.

It irked Buddy, also, that Macon cleaned his teeth with dental floss after every tequila. He sat there sliding the string up between his teeth and snapping it out, sliding it up, snapping it out, coiling the floss around his middle finger as he went. The way Dorene looked at his teeth.

Sometimes Macon would come early and hang around, strumming chords, thwacking out new songs on his guitar while Dorene trilled along. The cat would look up at Macon with its huge yellow eyes, stand on its hind legs and put its front paws against his knees. He'd take the little white paws in his hands, "Care to dance?" Macon would say, and Dorene would laugh laugh laugh.

Buddy felt he was always in her way. She got annoyed if she caught him "spying on her" while she danced to the radio, or "eavesdropping" while she talked on the phone. She bought a set of weights and Buddy did his best to ignore her, drinking beer, while she pumped her pectorals wearing a shortie nightgown. She warmed up by lifting three-pound dumbbells, then progressed to a twenty-pound barbell. Standing with her legs apart, she reminded Buddy of a gorgeous Amazon or one of the women on "American Gladiators," and some part of him pined for her. That was the thing. He noticed that he pined for her, missed her, when she was not around, but also, sometimes when she was.

Soon the rehearsals dragged on later and later into the night, and Dorene kept company with the band socially too. She saw so much of Macon Wells and the other musicians that more often than not, when Buddy came home from work, the apartment was empty. Because she seldom left a note, he found himself on tenterhooks for hours, waiting, wondering what she was up to. Sometimes he made them special dinners, only to find himself without an appetite, eating alone, when she didn't appear. It was a desolate, hope-wrecked time. Sitting there, pushing his food around his plate, he was embarrassed for himself. He had to distract his mind from what it knew, and his heart from what it was beginning to suspect. He took up training for a marathon bike race. Buddy wanted to ride in a century, which was a grueling hundred-mile road race he set the challenge of finishing in under six hours.

Buddy stayed late at work reading cycling magazines, gathering and comparing information on parts and products, and then he began to build his own frame. He chose steel over aluminum, carbon fiber or titanium because steel would give him the look he liked: graceful, thin tubes brazed into hand-filed lugs. Plus, it would be easier to repair if it broke. Rust was a problem, but the right paint would take care of that. Buddy welded together chrome-moly parts and, when he was finished, the fifty-six-centimeter frame weighed exactly four pounds, which was considered light for a solid, race-ready steel frame. He was proud. He added aero bars for speed and rigged a set of indexed shifters to the top so that he wouldn't have to get out of his aerodynamic position to change gears. Buddy intended to fly.

At first, he didn't train sensibly and he didn't care. Exhaustion was his primary goal and he chased it through dark streets and deserted parks until, bent over and sputtering for air, he caught it. Buddy had found a way to suffer he could take. He also discovered that, after a few hours of hard riding, his balls went numb and would stay that way for a couple more hours after he quit. This was an unexpected and added bonus that brought him some relief from wanting Dorene, waiting on her to come back.

Then, bit by bit, Buddy began to train properly. He followed a century training guide and rode eighty miles a week at first, with the goal of working his way up to almost two hundred miles a week after three months. He ate high-energy Power Bars, and drank Gatorade or toxic green Ultra Fuel. His body was a machine. He got leaner and stronger. His cooking changed too. He made only light, healthy recipes and became born-again about sprouts and carbohydrates. His diet was 65 percent carbohydrate, 20 percent fat and 15 percent protein. He knew that right before the century, he would carbo-load and digest at least 75 percent carbo. He could hardly stand to watch Dorene eat her usual cherry Pop-Tart and cups of instant coffee for breakfast. She refused to try his Müslix because it looked like birdseed.

The last weekend in August, Macon Wells and his band had a gig at Lone Star's. Dorene was exquisitely nervous. All day Friday she fussed, getting ready for that night. She put rollers in her hair to curl it, then dunked her head under the tap to wet it out straight again. She kept trying on clothes. She'd put things on and then rip them off herself as if they were obscene. Her notions of beauty changed radically from one moment to the next, and her confidence fluctuated too. She threw a leather bra-top she'd only recently bought in the trash. Just when she seemed to be pleased with the way she looked, she'd tear herself apart and start over from scratch.

Buddy left her briefly to go to the supermarket, where he'd won a Great Grub Grab contest, which entitled him to a thousand dollars' worth of free groceries, or as close to that as he could load into his shopping carts in the allotted five minutes. He arrived at the A & P twenty minutes early to case the place. His game plan was to start in the pasta aisle and move down to the meat counter after that. Olive oil was high on his list because it was eight dollars a bottle. The store's president posed with Buddy for a picture to go in the company newsletter, and then made an announcement over the P.A. to the shoppers, telling them the aisles would be roped off for five minutes for the Great Grub Grab and sorry for any inconvenience that caused. "Get the mops ready, boys!" he shouted and fired a little gun.

True to his intent, Buddy cleaned out the pasta shelves first. Then he grabbed anything he saw with "Fat-Free" or "No Cholesterol" stamped on the label. Running past amused shoppers, Buddy took out nearly every roast in the meat section, accounting for well over half his total. With the president counting down his final twenty seconds in five-second intervals, Buddy brought his third full cart down the frozen food aisle and, doing a huge double-take, skidded to a stop. He threw open the freezer door and started pitching tubs of Häagen-Dazs into the cart, which drew approving cheers from the mostly female crowd. When the cashier rang up the final total, Buddy had won $968.52 worth of free food, setting a Grub Grab record.

By the time he'd figured out where to put all the groceries, fitting the items in their cupboards and the freezer like he was doing a jigsaw puzzle, Dorene was ready for him to drive her to Lone Star's. The whole way there, she stared out the window singing to the radio, painting her nails bright pink, ignoring Buddy's small talk.

They arrived early. The band was setting up, carrying equipment in the bar's back door from a van, pushing dollies loaded with amps and coils of cable up onto the stage. There weren't any customers yet, although they were told it would get busy later on. Saturday night would be even busier, packed wall-to-wall. Colored lights were flashing above and across the stage. After a while, Macon plugged his guitar into an amp and twanged a loud chord. They went through a few songs to practice and check the sound. Buddy could tell Dorene was nervous, stiffer than he was used to her being, but she was good. Her voice was clear and full and she had the moves.

Altogether there were eight band members, the only women being the other two backup singers. They jumped down from the stage and came and sat at the tables crammed in near Buddy's. He heard names from time to time; there were no formal introductions. Bev and Paulette were the singers, but he didn't know who was who, thought he did, but got it wrong. The drummer was Rude Blake, then there was Howlie Rollins, Leebert Smith, Chook Hudson—Buddy gave up trying to get them straight. The thing was, he didn't have to, because nobody talked to him. They argued amiably about the music industry, the doubtful longevity of CDs, amplifiers, polyps, and left Buddy out of it.

People began to come in and the empty tables filled up. Music cranked out of the P.A. speakers to set the tone for the night, warm the crowd. People were shouting to each other, the air got thick and fogged with smoke. Buddy tried to catch Dorene's eye but she was involved in a serious discussion with the other singers, their knees kissing. Mute as a strip of wallpaper, he drank glass after glass of Wild Turkey and hated himself for it. It would smirch his training. He didn't care. He watched with some interest as Dorene reinvented herself. He went to use the john and, when he came back, Macon Wells was onstage with the band. There was a screech of feedback and Macon welcomed everybody to Lone Star's and told them to drink up since they were getting a cut of the bar tab. Dance if they wanted to. Then the band started playing.

Buddy watched people get up to dance, jostle themselves around the jammed floor. He kept drinking until, by the time the set ended and the band took a break, he'd lost all power of locomotion and his hand only flopped in his lap when Dorene came and held hers out for a high five.

"They like me," she told him, pressing a soda bottle against her cheek. She looked like she'd been basking in the hot sun. She waved to somebody. "I'm part of the group. A band can be kind of a family. So—how was I? I'm dying to know what you think."

Buddy tried to loosen up his tongue to speak, but after not

saying a single word all night, he'd lost that ability too. He licked his lips, which felt as numb and ungainly as swim flippers.

"Whelper?" Dorene said, really looking at him for the first time.

Buddy couldn't quite focus on her and he tried to pull his head back to see if that made any difference, which caused his body to lurch like he was on a bike that had hit a rut and spun out of control. Whoa, he said or thought, hold on.

"Gee, are you all right?" Dorene asked, peering at him, eyeball to eyeball.

There was no simple answer to that question. Buddy knew that Dorene was beautiful and full of spunk. That was what he knew. He thought, *you never know a real good thing until she says good-bye.* It was a line from a song.

When Buddy woke up the next morning, he lay for a long moment uncertain if he'd be able to move. He didn't remember getting home. His brain pounded, his back ached. When he managed to raise himself into a semi-upright position, he sat holding his head in his hands while his neck protested the new posture violently. Dorene was still asleep beside him. He got himself standing and found that not only was he hung over, he was still a little drunk. He wove his way into the kitchen, where he cracked a raw egg into a glass of fruit-punch-flavored Gatorade and drank it.

In the bathroom, Buddy took a long hot shower, leaning against the wall tiles for support. When he got out, he swallowed a handful of aspirins, brushed his teeth and shaved off his goatee. Saturday was the most important day of the week as far as his century training program went. It was the day he rode the longest distance, increasing his miles and endurance week by week. He was scheduled to bike sixty miles, which would take him about four hours if he was in top condition. Buddy put on his space-age biking gear. He marveled at the complex, man-made fibers designed to be supremely functional and wind-resistant and to actively wick perspiration away from the body to keep the rider cool. He wore a neon-pink Coolmax jersey, black Lycra shorts, yellow Lycra gloves, silver mirror Killer Loop glasses, special cycling shoes with cleats that attached to his clipless pedals, and a Bell Pro Razor helmet with pump-action by Reebok to let him fine-tune it, on the road, for a custom fit. Buddy taped a flashing red reflector to the back of his helmet to act as a conspicuous tail-light.

Buddy left Dorene a note telling her he'd meet her at Lone Star's later, and even though he didn't feel like it, went out for his long ride. He was building his stamina. Buddy hoped there was an equivalent to the famed runner's high, which he thought must be similar to an orgasm, that he might be lucky enough to experience. He'd felt something once, a kind of buzzing sensation on the top of his head that then cascaded down his body. It had been pretty good. Buddy found his pace and, after a while, the hangover subdued. He was a high-tech Lone Ranger riding his trusty chrome-moly steed into the sunset. Buddy kept going when his legs got rubbery because he knew he would get a second wind. When it came, distance—long distance—seemed not only possible but essential.

Buddy rode straight to Lone Star's that night and chained his bike to a tree in front. The cleated shoes were easier to leave locked into the jaws of the pedals, so he slipped his feet out, took off his socks and walked barefoot into the bar. It probably was against the rules, but nobody stopped him. A lot of people looked like they wanted to, but nobody did. Buddy's face and hair were soaked with sweat and he shook himself dry the way a dog does. The bar was jam-packed and loud. An opening band was getting the crowd fired up. Dorene was already backstage with Macon and the other musicians, fixing her clothes and makeup. The first band finished to thundering applause, people yelled and rapped their glasses on the tables. Buddy ordered a club soda with lime. He ordered a second, and then Macon Wells took the stage and Dorene started singing. She was where she'd always wanted to be. She was perfect.

Buddy knew that Dorene didn't need him anymore. He'd made an honest mistake. He'd confused need and longing with love. He'd done his best to help her and had grown used to taking care of her. He'd enjoyed it for a while and she'd come to rely on his support. They were in it together, but the whole thing was flawed. It was based on unhappiness. They depended on Dorene's misery and, now that she wasn't sad or desperate, Buddy was useless. It had happened naturally enough and maybe it was even common for unhappy need such as that to pass for love. They were foul-weather friends, only. It wasn't healthy or right.

When the set ended, Buddy stood up beside his table. Dorene went to the bar and got a drink, mingled first, talking to people before she came over. The music tape was playing again and the whole place rocked with sound. She looked energized, blissfully happy, the lights roiled the tobacco smoke into dreamy swirls above her head. She was just about to say something to Buddy when she saw he was holding his bicycle helmet, and whatever it was got stuck in her throat. Her eyes searched him. They went back and forth across his face, and he knew at least he would not have to tell her he was leaving.

"Oh, Whelper," she said, slumping into a chair.

"It's just," Buddy said, "that I'm used to living on my own. I prefer it. When I live with someone, I lose myself in the deal. I take one step forward, two steps back. I don't like the way I act."

"I'm so sorry, Whelper. I never meant—"

"At least the fridge is stocked," Buddy said. "There's a lot for you to eat."

"Ice cream," Dorene said. "My favorite." And Buddy could tell she was getting ready to throw her arms around him. It was the last thing he could let her do. He put on his pump-action helmet with the pulsating reflector and walked out, his bared feet supple and springy as a newborn's.

TWENTY-TWO

MIDWAY HOME, Buddy stopped and dialed Cheryl's number.

"Cheryl, I want—" he said.

"I can't talk now, Buddy, I'm flustered. Toomer's got his little girl, Roseanne, here. I think I told you about her. She's adorable. We were playing Twister and now I'm just making us some peanut butter and pineapple sandwiches to eat in the backyard for a picnic. You should see Toomer. He gives happy a new meaning. His face, when Roseanne put her arms around his neck and whispered some little secret meant only for his ears, is something I won't ever forget. She called him Daddy once, but I don't think he heard her that time. Life is so full of near misses that could make or break a person's day. Every hour is a lottery you either win or lose."

"Cheryl," Buddy said. "I won't be calling you anymore. I won't be pestering you in the future."

"You don't pester me, Buddy. I'd tell you if you did. What's wrong?"

"I just thought I wouldn't call you anymore."

"Call me if you want."

"I don't know. I don't have much to say."

"So? I'm not complaining. It's fine with me, if you don't mind. Who cares? It's your phone bill. Anyway, we can't all be big mouths. Look at Toomer. His lips are sealed most of the time. But you have to know he tries hard in his own way, and when he does say something, I listen. I just hope Roseanne will grow up hearing him too. We all ought to poke the wax out of our ears and fine-tune our hearing so we don't miss the important stuff, which is never said as loud as we'd like."

"I might call, then," Buddy said.

"Call if you want," Cheryl said and hung up.

Buddy drove on. Later, at the warehouse lot, he switched the mini-bus back for his pickup. The VCRs were gone and the cab smelled of hair spray. Buddy opened the windows to air it out. He drove, without direction he thought, until he ended up parked by the roadside zoo. He sat for a long time in the pickup before he got out and crossed the tall grass to BoBo's cage.

The black bear was hunched as usual against the farthest bars of the cage, occupied with something moving in the straw between its feet, unaffected by the glistening drool hanging from its mouth. A bony woman in a frilly dress was taking pictures of it, and she kept backing up, trying to get all of the bear in her viewfinder. Finally she tucked up the bottom of her dress, crouched and snapped off a couple of shots. She had an instant camera that spit the pictures out front, and she pulled each photograph from it and kept looking from the pictures to the bear in its cage.

"I don't know," she said, flapping the pictures at Buddy. "These things cost, and I figure maybe that bear is not so photogenic. I wish they had colored parrots or a leopard at least with spots. That bear is introverted. I don't know why I'm wasting my time. I wanted a picture of a live bear to give to my nephew, but I know what he would think. He'd think I just handed him more disappointment, which he doesn't need in his life at the moment. Where's the danger, he'd ask? That bear has nothing going for him, he'd say. That bear is a loser. At his age, understatement is ridiculous. I'm going to forget it and take him a baseball bat, or something in tissue paper he can unwrap." She handed Buddy the pictures and walked away.

Buddy leafed through them. Mostly they were hard to make out, the bear seeming a kind of shadow of itself, deep in its own background. He tucked the pictures in his shirt pocket and went to work on the lock. The bear watched him with nothing much in its eyes. The lock was stiff and rusted but didn't take that long to break off with pliers. Buddy swung open the door and jumped back out of the way. When the bear didn't move, Buddy banged on the metal with the palm of his hand. He closed the door almost shut and swung it open again to show the bear what it meant—an open door. The bear came forward but paused on the threshold, looking around with the whole of its head as though it expected a trick or an ambush. Buddy looked around too. "Go on," he said, "get yourself the fuck out of—" But before he could finish, the bear lunged out of the cage on all fours and hit Buddy square in the chest, knocking him to the ground. The bear's front legs buckled under and it rolled on top of Buddy and they lay entangled for a moment, the two of them, their arms wrapped around one another, before the bear swiped a gash across Buddy's neck as it pulled up off him.

Buddy smelled the rotten, musky stench of the bear's fur, felt the blood leaving the gash in his neck, the ground shuddering with the bear's weight as it gained momentum and rhythm came to its running. Buddy heaved up on his elbows with a groan and turned onto his stomach to watch. The bear bolted for the highway or maybe it was for the woods beyond, across two lanes of traffic. As the bear hit the pavement at full speed, Buddy started yelling, although there were no words to what he said. He saw the truck, and the bear with its vision set on the distant greenery. There was a thud, softer than he'd have thought. Buddy looked away before the bear came down, while it was still up against sky, its front feet beating the wind like something wild.

Months went by before Buddy got over feeling that no matter what he was doing, something was missing, that he should be doing something else. Still, he tried to push any thoughts of a young woman knocking on his door, and then taking off her clothes, from his mind. Loneliness was a place he knew his way around. He wasn't scared of its dark corners. He spent his time reading bicycling magazines, planning the century races across the country he would enter. There was the Blue Ridge Brutal 100 in North Carolina, El Tour de Tucsón in Arizona and the Hotter 'n Hell Hundred in Texas, for starters. Buddy still had some training to do, but he figured, even now, at least he'd be able to finish. He had a route he liked, with a tree he rode by that looked as though it could have been struck by lightning, more than once.

This book is set in Garamond, a standard typeface used by book designers and printers for four centuries, and one of the finest old styles ever cut. Some characteristics of Garamond to note are the small spur on the "G," the open bowl on the "P," the curving tail on the "R," and the short lower-case height and very small counters of the "a" and "e."

The text stock is
55 lb. Windsor High-bulk Cream

Printed in Canada by
Friesen Printers